MOWING THE CEMETERY

Stories From A Northern Town

by

John Solensten

line drawings by
Robert Walton

Lone Butte Press

Other books by John Solensten

The Heron Dancer, New Rivers Press, 1981

Good Thunder, State University of New York Press, 1983.

There Lies a Fair Land, edited by John Solensten, New Rivers Press, 1985

ISBN 0-945455-00-3
Publisher— Lone Butte Press
        P.O. Box 3246
        Fargo, N.D. 58108

ACKNOWLEDGMENTS

"The Romantic Undertaker" was published in *There Lies A Fair Land* in 1985 by New Rivers Press and is reprinted with permission.

"Love the Wild Swan" was previously published in *Plainswoman* and is reprinted with permission.

"Two: A Story of Numbers" was previously published in *Stiller's Pond* by New Rivers Press and is reprinted with permission.

"Children of Light" was previously published in *Northland Review* and is reprinted with permission.

Forward

It was logical that of all the restless young men in my hometown I would be hired to mow the cemetery during the summer. I was born a caretaker—one of those serious young men with what used to be called "ministerial tendencies."

The cemetery itself was a neatly-trimmed, slightly rolling meadow—a patchwork of plots and stones and lingering sad bouquets laid in the middle of cornfields intense with sun and growth and the richness of Midwestern soil. Mowing it was serious, deaconlike business. It had to be done with a certain respect. Somehow, someone had to forgive the use of a power mower.

But I would not have you believe that mowing the place was a morbid occupation. Well, yes, there were funerals and I turned off the mower and sat a polite distance away and heard words of dust and resurrection flutter on the wind like evanescent gray birds, but all in all it was a lively place—a place where people often shared snapshot memories with me. Cars rolled in and people stepped out into the sun with shears and flowers and a quiet cheerfulness. For awhile they dutifully fretted about the monuments and grass. And then sometimes they would tell me stories— stories that defined them and the people "gone ahead to glory or something," as one of them put it. These stories were like old photos turned sideways to put the people in them back into the flow of life and events. It was a strangely joyful and communal experience listening to those stories.

For we are all stories—all of us. All of us want to be noticed, to be talked about. These are stories of people back there, down the road, across town. I've tried to let people in these stories speak like themselves, for themselves; and the voices often speak across individual stories like echoic voices from summer porches and rooms within the houses.

Oh, it's not so easygoing as all that, of course. There are those odd and wild and eccentric ones—my uncle, for instance—the mayor of the town—the myth man of the county—bigger than life—in his own private fury about life. My hometown was tolerant of eccentricity. On city streets today that eccentricity might be called madness, I suppose.

Odin is not on any map. If there is a town of that name, disregard the connection. Odin is the town we all put together in our collective memories. It's our town because in those memories we all put our own people in it. It can also be the town we're living in right now—seen through our eyes—our special vision.

It's our town.

John Solensten

The Mayor

When Harold Liv, DDS, set up his dental practice one spring day in the old First State Bank building in Odin, there was a lot of muttering and shaking of heads and gossip.

It was the building itself, partly. John Magnuson (Banker Magnuson, they called him) had had it built in the Greek revival style in 1905—had it built with pink granite shipped on the Great Lakes from Vermont. Raised it up in scaled-down grandeur right in the middle of scrub pine and aspen and poplar. No use to talk "indigenous" to him. When Louis Sullivan came all the way up to Odin on a train and showed Magnuson other plans, Magnuson (they say) rolled the plans up, stuck them in Sullivan's pocket and said, "I don't give a damn for all those plants hanging in the lobby and carved on the brick. We don't play ring-around-the-rosy out here; we want something that stays—something even a Yankee can take his hat off to—something solid as a rock."

The bank was solid all right. It survived the Great Depression and a few crop failures and the coming of new banks to the county. But when Magnuson died, the bank examiners found a lot of irregularities and then there was a new, modern bank at Grand Marais, six miles away, so that was the end of it as a bank. Then nobody would buy the building—not even the Sons of Norway or the Masons. So it sat there a long time, frowning down on the town with its low, deep-browed pediment, its marble columns weathering gray-green while the Lake Superior wind, the elegist, hummed sadly through its broken windows.

Nobody would buy it except Dr. Liv. The real estate man, Jim Nelson, said Liv walked in and saw the oak carving the Germans did in the lobby and said something about "the glory that was Greece" instead of asking about taxes and heating and such things and bought it just like that. Then Liv closed off everything except four conference rooms, converting them to a bedroom, a waiting room and his two dental chair rooms.

The jokes followed. In the Square Deal Cafe down the street from the bank men turned their big white coffee cups around and around and around, examining them carefully before they said, "You wait till you get his bill; then you'll see why the bank," or, "If you send your wife to that tall man who hasn't got one, sit close by, tell her no gas and watch what cavity he fills."

The real estate man tried to dispel some of the rumors. He said, turning his coffee cup around and around, "Why he bought it for what he paid for three years' rent in Chicago. Where did you want him to go? Into the feed store?"

Chicago—where Sullivan had come from. That was another thing that made it hard for people to believe it. For years the people in Odin tried to get a doctor to come out from Duluth or Minneapolis. Once, a young doctor, fresh out of med school, came out to look the town over but his wife wouldn't even get out of the car to look at anything or talk to anyone.

So why a dentist—a good dentist—from Chicago—the East to north country people? Liv told the real estate man that he was sent out by a national dentists' organization, but that didn't explain anything really. It might as well have been a missionary organization. Duluth Dentist Supply had the Duluth Credit Bureau check Liv out before giving him credit for dental supplies. (He had two big new blue dental chairs sent out from Chicago.) Nothing there. All P's for prompt payment; wife deceased; former address in the Wrigley Building. Nothing to chew on there.

What to do? Well, try him out in broad daylight. Give him a chance. Mrs. Aamot went to Liv first—the pastor's wife, a daring woman who played the violin in church and then (that was going too far) the guitar. "Well?" people asked her later, "...what do you think of our new dentist Liv?"

And she replied, "He is better than any dentist I had in Minneapolis." "Minneapolis?" they said. "Well, well...Minneapolis, you say...."

Liv was a tall man with a great ruddy nose, an arching freckled forehead, blue eyes and thick red hair combed back straightly and neatly. In his office he wore immaculate, starched white jackets washed and ironed by a laundry in Two Harbors.

He was a good dentist but he never kidded anyone about being painless. "Pain tells us what we need to know sometimes," he told his patients. Once they were in the chair kids didn't make a move, not a move. And still, he had a gentle touch.

"Why is it when Doc Liv puts a bib on you and leans you back and asks how you are, it's better than any barber giving a hot shave and all of it," Jim Nelson used to ask, and somone would answer, "How should I know?"

Still there was the old bank and the jokes to reckon with. But he reassured the people very quickly that his charges were reasonable. Not only that but because he was alone in that big office he hardly got around to billing anyone. He only sent out one bill with a thanks on the bottom of it. No follow-up. That meant, "Pay me last" to most people or, "Pay me if you can" to others.

Evenings he would walk downtown—always in a fine suit—brown or blue or tan—and nod to everyone and eat dinner at the Square Deal Cafe and go back to that building. He kept the common touch, but he never played cards or shot pool or such things. Nobody would think to ask him to. Evenings he would walk downtown and then go back to that building. Just before dark he would be standing there on the portico of the building with his hands behind his back. What was he looking at? The East. The East? Yes, the East. Then he would go back inside and the lights would go off. Kids tried to peep inside the building but it wasn't any use. It was a bank. You had to *be* inside to *see* inside.

There were times when he took his black Buick out and went somewhere, driving so fast no one ever quite figured out his destination. The car was an old Roadmaster he had bought from an estate sale. The windows were cloudy-opaque from sitting out in a machine shed so long. Farmers working in the fields waved at him but he was too busy driving to wave back. The only person who drove as fast as he did was the Lutheran pastor.

He had other strange habits too—like wearing boots with pointed toes and never taking them off for anything—anything. That's why he never bowled, people guessed. He would have to take the boots off and put on bowling shoes. But was there something wrong with his feet? Could it be that—? No. No. Superstitions. Nonsense.

It was his mysterious Chicago connection that got him elected mayor. Somebody he knew there bought the bond issue so the town could rebuild the sewage plant and put in street lighting. Nobody in Minnesota would—

even at fifteen years and eight percent. Before that, people had said, "The town is really dying now. It's dark and it even smells like it's dying and nobody's ever going to build here again." People in little towns—especially old people—may *think* dying but they never *say* it.

But a bond brokerage in Chicago bought all of the Odin bond issue. The acceptance letter, posted at the town hall, said, "We base our acceptance of this issue on our good opinion of the ability of industrious people living on good land to repay the issue through the special assessment schedule specified and we wish to thank Dr. Harold Liv, a former Chicagoan and now a successful local dentist, for his recommendations in this matter."

It may have been as sentimental and schmaltzy as an old James Stewart movie but a lot of people in town walked down to the bank building the evening after the letter of acceptance came and stood there quietly and when Liv came out of the shadows of the Doric columns shook his hand one by one. No singing "He's a Jolly Good Fellow" or anything like that. Afterward everyone went home quietly.

A few people who had given up and were moving to Duluth or Minneapolis laughed at the whole thing and said it only postponed the inevitable. But people who wanted to stay or had to stay began to have a new faith. There is a terrible thing about sewage and darkness in a little town. People learn to tolerate being close all the time and gossiping all the time, but sewage—. And the darkness—it seems to give the grass, the long grass, more power and more mystery at night so the houses seem to settle in it like things being swallowed gradually. Sometimes at the edge of town people had added an extra row of cement blocks on a foundation when they built a house just to keep it above the grass.

There is usually some special place where people feel they belong. It's something people feel that says, "Why not here? It's as good as anyplace." Or it's other things. "I remember when my father was putting a new roof on that porch and fell off and we thought he was dead but he got up and laughed and went up the ladder again."

Dr. Liv understood it—the connection between people and the land—and he came to celebrate it. And the people, knowing that, made him mayor—less than a year after he came—296 votes to 67 by official count. The swearing-in ceremony took place in the gym of the old brownstone elementary school on the north end of town. It was a beautiful February night. People tried to forget the groaning of the wind through the big transoms over the rows of chairs and there was a short speech by Al

Hanson, the owner of the Gamble store. Hanson said, "This man Doc Liv came down out of that high tower in Chicago and came out to God's own country to try to make his fortune. And now he already owns the bank [laughter], has been elected mayor [laughter] and has helped people here on both ends of their lives [nervous laughter] with his sewers and his dental chairs...." That was Hanson's speech.

When Liv stood up with his big face and smiled a cool thin smile, everything got quiet. His eyes were so bright they always seemed to be looking right at people. He spoke softly so people had to lean into the words. "Thank you!" he said, "but don't expect too much of me. I came here to practice dentistry and to breathe good clean air again. I think we all want to stay here and dream and build and hold on because it was hard for the first people to come here and stay here a long time ago. I feel that deeply, but don't expect me to explain it, it's in my gut. Thank you, but don't expect too much of me."

"That's pretty modest ain't it, Mr. Mayor?" Hanson said. Like everyone else he was surprised and had expected something more, but Liv only smiled and nodded and sat down again. It was a little tense for a while but there was plenty of food and coffee and everybody began to eat quietly until somebody said very loudly, "Well, I don't say much to him when he's got a drill in my mouth and he sure isn't a drag-out speaker either." Dr. Liv laughed and smiled and the dinner was a glad winter feast. People talked so loudly the wind in the transom faded and the big room warmed and glowed as if there were new fires in people's hearts.

And Dr. Liv *was* a fine dentist—quick, careful, thorough. Faces looked better; people talked better; children smiled metal bands and rows of lead-silver braces and thought about being prettier or handsomer. The lights burned into the night in the old bank building and four new families came to Odin to work at the big Co-Op garage and store—four new families, twenty-six people. And whole families—old and new—began to come to Liv's office for dental work.

Then, suddenly, on a spring day the madness began—his madness or a madness he caught somewhere and somehow—a week of it, that left a lot of people a little crazy too.

All through the year—except for that week in spring—Dr. Liv was a man of order and punctuality. His eyes were open and clear as summer sunshine and people who had appointments for 9:15 on a Tuesday morning got in at 9:15 on Tuesday morning. Even if he was not finished with another patient, Liv would put the next patient into his number two baby blue dentist's chair and start the Novocain or put in a clamp or something. Nobody in town was ever really in that much of a hurry but they liked the way he handled them—so much better than the dentists in Duluth, who kept patients waiting for hours and never apologized. When 12:00 came, Dr. Liv walked outside (a patient was usually leaving for lunch if he or she could chew), looked up at the sky and then walked briskly to the Square Deal Cafe. Mrs. Hagen who runs the cafe got so used to his punctuality that she could start a steak and pop in the toast and take the cellophane off a salad and practically have his Tuesday steak sandwich special there in the booth when he sat down. Nobody joined him in the booth. He nodded and smiled at everyone but that booth was the mayor's and the mayor and the dentist kept a busy schedule.

But nosy people began to see a few funny things. First of all, Dr. Liv rarely got mail from anywhere except Duluth and Two Harbors and other towns like that—bills mostly. Once a year income tax things but nothing else. It was as if nobody knew he was living in Odin or didn't care. And he had no winter clothes. Twenty below and colder than a witch's et cetera and he would walk down to lunch wearing only a suit and tie—no coat. People said that whenever he went someplace he would warm up the old Buick Roadmaster until he could sit in it without a coat. And then he drove off to someplace so fast it was almost impossible to follow him.

And then spring came, one of those days when the Indian flowers riot in the ditches and the earth groans and gulls pivot and wing, screaming above the wet slabs of black plowing in the little northern fields. On that day, the word would get around town. "He's not meeting his afternoon appointments. We waited forty minutes. Nothing locked up, you know. Just nobody there." Some of the older people coming in for appointments were frightened when they saw Dr. Liv had propped up his white jacket, stuffed with newspaper, in the main chair and put a plastic skull full of big teeth on top of it. That *was* scary.

But later that week Dr. Liv showed up all over the countryside. If some of the reports could be believed he was ubiquitous. Some people saw him in a green zip-tight suit whistling through his fingers. Others saw him wearing a black soft-brimmed hat and a white canvas shirt open at the neck and a pair of heavy brown trousers. He was everywhere that week and yet no one could agree where or when. Odin, and the whole county, have a population of less than 5000. In town, everybody knows everyone else's affairs. Marks are put nine months later on calendars when young people marry. There are no secrets. And yet, even though dozens of people saw Dr. Liv—or claimed to have seen him—they would never say what they did then or what he did or said. "I saw him," or "I seen him...down by the ..." people would say, a faraway thin smile on their faces. And that was it. They would walk away or change the subject.

After that week—on Monday morning at 8:30 promptly to be exact—Dr. Liv would be in his office again in his white dentist's coat, his eyes blue as sky polished by new sun. The people might come into the office reluctantly at first, but the lights were bright and clear and his smile so gentle they would always say "Good morning, again Dr. Liv" and then allow themselves to be seated in one of the blue chairs. His work was precise and impeccable. He explained everything carefully. "Goodbye again, Dr. Liv," the patients would say, adding, "send me a bill." At 12:00 he would stand for a moment on the portico of the bank building, pull out that thick old Hamilton watch, glance at it and descend the stairs with the slight limp he always had. Monday it was. His roast beef dinner would be in the booth at the Square Deal Cafe when he sat down. "Good morning again, Doc," the other people would say to him. "Good morning again," he would say to them. And Mrs. Hagen, the owner of the Square Deal Cafe, would smile and smile—with her new dentures.

As weeks and weeks rolled by, people became more and more suspicious. "Where are the street lights?" people asked each other. They never asked Dr. Liv himself.

"When are they going to start digging the new sewer plant?" they complained, but never directly to him.

"Go ask the Mayor yourself," somebody would say to someone else and that person would say, "I can't do that. He fixed every tooth in the family and I only sent him ten dollars this year."

No lights, no sewage system. The man began to trouble the people in Odin. Who was he really? Somebody from another time, another place? The Devil himself with strange feet? No, no, don't say that. He gets bored out here and has to raise a little hell. He never hurt anyone, never took after anyone's wife. He's got a weakness maybe—Jack Daniels to be specific—but none of us is perfect—that's for sure. And he is a church-goer. Well, funerals at least. No, he is a man of moods and maybe some deep grief—a solitary man of sorrows as the Bible says, so live and let live.

Still, a small voice says, deep in the heart, he is not quite here while he is here and he will probably go away to God knows where in that black Buick of his, you wait and see. He said in that speech of his not to expect too much and I guess he meant it.

Meanwhile, he paid his bills and gave the town something and someone it had never had before. The bank building stood at the end of Main Street looking things over like it, too, was waiting to see what was going to happen.

Wilderness

Olafson sat on the back steps of the house where he took a room each July in town on the north shore of Lake Superior and looked out into a stand of ancient cedars ranging up the hill and into the big forest. A ragged lawn, embroidered with Indian paintbrush, lay between him and the edge of the trees. The sun, rising on his right, was warmly benevolent....

And yet it happened again—the something that caught his heart like a claw and then suddenly released it into quick staccato beats of fear. It was silly and irrational—especially for an educated man. Yet—wildernesses—unnamed things—were there in the cedars again. He coughed; coughed again; heard his own heart beat. The heart, says an old Yiddish proverb, is half a prophet.

He tried to resist it. There was something happening, but he did not wish to be in the *pragma*, the plot. To teach literature is one thing; to be in such a story is another. Yet someone or something was writing it already—the story. He sat, looking out into the stand of cedars, and coughed and looked angrily at the cigarette in his hand and snapped it away. The sun rose higher. Let the day come.

Sitting there, he could hear the metallic pulsing of her typewriter. There was her house—square, white, tall-windowed and very Prussian. At attention always, not an unkempt bush or tree within two hundred feet of it. The typing? Already she was writing, sitting sternly upright at the ancient Smith-Corona machine, her gnarl-brown hands working slowly, because she was arthritic. A cane was hooked on the edge of a nearby chair. Her long face was rigid and mottled brown and white, except for the vibrant blue eyes. She did an article for a learned journal every three months. She was published and she was read. He was not published much; hardly read. Diminuendo.

He thought about visiting her—even disrupting her. He visited her only once in awhile, and then preferred to sit outside on her concrete veranda because it was easier to get away from her out there—especially if the mosquitoes became fierce. When she held court on the veranda she always demanded his complete attention. When she was ready to sit down he would have to lift that long skeletal leg—the right one—up on a footstool and put a little soiled pillow under it. Then he had to wait on her and get the coffee and the musty pastries and the copies of *Der Spiegel* and put them on the coffee table. When they were both settled, she began her monologue, her voice lisping heavily in that special way people of old German families lisp.

Then he sat; listened, listened some more. Her primary subject was bad help and then it was the maltreatment of professors in America. "They think, somehow, they are merely subsidizing our hobbies," she would say. "In Germany, professors are held in esteem and paid well. Here— except for the business ones—they are considered to be hired men and hired women."

And then her heart condition. Her heart condition. Not enough exercise, et cetera. (That et cetera was lisped very humorously.) Yet in the resonance of her bones—in the subtle redolence of dust from rooms full of old things—he began to hear his own history in prophecy. Had he not grown up believing that he was born with a memory—a memory of what the older ones knew? He listened and he knew her. And from time to time he glanced at the piano inside the house through a patio window and saw her pictures and her young silver face in the silver frame. She was beautiful then and he reluctantly acknowledged that he—of that time and place—might even have loved her and moved toward the end with her in her history—sister, lover in another time, but now an ancient one—angular and something else. She, her hair in silver shields, held him in stone silence. Dear God! What does it mean to love an old woman's bones?

He had never heard her sing, but he heard words of her songs when he looked at the ebony piano.... He drifted—as he often did when he was with her. She had outrageous notions sometimes. The Austrian pines behind her house for example. Why cut them for Christmas trees? Pot them and replant them in the spring...and then she stood behind the first and last potted one in her living room—in a kind of vague and piny embrace—her blue eyes burning at him so fiercely he looked down and saw, then, the first dead needles. And after she had it set outside it sat at the edge of the woods until July—a sere reminder of he-didn't-know-what....

Sitting there again in his thoughts on the steps of his rented place, he pulled his own bony ass and legs around into a comfortable position and sipped his coffee. He liked his own hiking smell—sweet, sticky pine and earth. No more wearing jeans to class though. As Dean Brunner said, assistant professor Olafson listening, sitting in his jeans there in the coffee lounge, "Jeans are no longer quite appropriate. Some of us see them as a symbol of the chaotic juvenilism of the 70's." The graying of academe.

The Indian—a Chippewa she called Todd—was supposed to come at seven that morning to do the lawn. He never came at seven. He came earlier on a bright day; later on a dark one. He had his own history, his own rhythm and pulse.

Oh, but Todd *was* coming from somewhere up the hill, the loud exhaust of his old green pickup truck popping and farting as he probably was, behind him fishing gear and the long shovels jiggling in the truck box.

The quarrel would take place in about ten minutes and she would lose it. It would interrupt her work. Olafson's had not begun, so he could listen. She knew he was listening—counted on him to listen.

Todd was suddenly there in the middle of the lawn looking at the grass, his hands on his stomach, his round face gleaming with something but certainly not sweat.

She limped out through the back screen door and stood behind Todd like a field marshal reviewing troops, the heels of both hands resting on her cane. He turned and began unloading a hand lawn mower—the kind with a reel in it and no motor.

"Good morning, Todd!" she exclaimed cheerfully so Olafson could hear. "Are you ready for a good morning's work?"

He was pulling a rake through the front window of the pickup. She smiled gray teeth at him, trying to be "populist," as she called it.

"I always do a good morning's work," he said. "I rest when I'm tired, but I work hard too, but not in a crazy way."

He bent over the mower, his bare back slipping out of pants and shirt.

She poked at him with that cane. He turned, eyes steady, and said, "I saw that cane in half."

False cheerfulness. "Oh, but I don't want you to do that. I want you to cut about six feet of brush and trees away back there at the edge of the woods."

She nodded vaguely toward Olafson and then winked. He nodded in return, then looked at his own shoes. "I'm no lumberjack," he said. "I cut grass and weeds."

"So you won't?"

"No I won't," he said, bending over at the mower, pumping oil from an old copper oilcan that popped and wheezed under his thumb.

Now she was in a fix. She knew Todd had a family and needed the money he got for doing her yard. And professors are enlightened—yes—and even liberal people.

"Maybe there's something I don't understand," she said, her words lisping more quietly.

"Oh," he said, "there's not much more to understand," kneeling again to adjust the old mower, "I cut grass and weeds. No trees like those."

"Is it your love of the woods?"

No answer—just the whir of that ancient mower working, the grass clipping off in arcs full of green needles and the heads of Indian paintbrushes.

"I can't do a thing with you, can I?" she cried. Then, hobbling in pain, she moved slowly back to the veranda where on a white table she placed eight dollars in an envelope under a little steel claw used for weeding flower beds.

Olafson went back inside the rooming house to look at his notes again and to allow his colleagues' words to haunt him briefly. "Why are you going where there's no library?" they asked. "You'll miss the Beach lecture," they warned. Teaching. There's no rest in it. If you aren't reading, you should be. If you aren't writing you may perish indeed. Writing, however, is an unnatural act. It may do things to your body.

He looked at what he had done the day before. That was a good way to get going. "Time and Tragic Rhythm in Hedda Gabler." He was going to do a reader response thing and use Northrup Frye—the mythos of autumn. It had better work. It had better be PMLA stuff. You can't be an assistant professor forever: if you are, you may not be allowed to be a professor at all. It was all a series of unnatural acts. She—Professor von Fange—said she ruined her hip sitting at the typewriter doing her dissertation. Olafson was not sure what—besides one marriage—he was ruining, but there was surely something ticking in his mortal body somewhere.

He focused on Scene One in which autumn leaves are seen through a window on the veranda of the Tesman home.

Knocking on the door behind him.

"Who is it?"

"The phone."

"What does the phone want?" he asked. Oh, shit, Mrs. Hammer doesn't think you're clever, he told himself. He found the phone lying there on the hall table—a black inert thing—a totem of Mrs. Hammer.

"Hello."

"Hello...." It was she. No, he told himself. I will not interrupt my writing to cut any goddam brush.

"...do you see them?"

"See what?"

"They somehow make me ill."

"What?"

"They are making a fiendish racket, too. Please. Just look in my back yard and come over for a minute."

"All right."

He hung up and walked down the hall and out the back door into the yard.

My God what a noise. There, high on the beards of the cedars at the back of her yard, fifty or so crows were perched or flying about cawing and screaming, their oil-slick feathers glistening in the midmorning sun.

He looked for Todd. He and his truck were gone.

Where was the professor? He cut through Mrs. Hammer's garden rows and saw no one. He walked over toward the professor's veranda.

Oh, she stood outlined behind her screen door—her gray form held back from the opening as if dissolving from a vague photograph. He walked toward her, yelling at the crows over his shoulder. "Beat it, you black devils!"

She was shaking in there—her whole body. He stood there trying to see her clearly.

"As you can understand," she mumbled, "they frighten me. They are punctual as he is not."

"He?"

"The yard man. You see, I don't even like his name."

"I'll get rid of them," Olafson said.

"You can't shoot a gun in town."

"I have some cherry bombs...."

"No bombs...." The voice shaking.

"Firecrackers...."

"Oh, please!" she cried. She was turning to go back through regions of books and magazines to her typewriter. "They come at exactly 10:30," she called back at him over her shoulder. "They wish to take me from my work, I think."

He turned.

They were silent above him. Then their black choirs began their raucous litanies again. They somehow made him sick too as he stood there.

He went to his car—the black chorus taunting at his back. In the trunk were a few cherry bombs from the Fourth of July—boyish things. Also, somewhere in there, a slingshot.

The idea was fiendishly clever and Poesque. Light a cherry bomb and shoot it into the trees. Pow! Easy for an old mortar man—a Nam man.

He lit a cigarette; fixed a cherry bomb carefully in the leathery patch; pulled back; lit the cherry bomb; and fired.

A burst in the trees right in the midst of them.

They disappeared slyly—slipped off the trees, dipping down into deep woods—evasive as Cong. You never get them, you never stop them. Erase them and they write themselves again on another sky, in another clearing.

She was calling him from her door. He walked over to her. "That was heroic," she said, "and I am indebted to you."

She opened the screen door slightly and handed him a single orange blossom—a tiger lily—and he took it. It bent in a silly way over his wrist.

"If they come back," her hollow voice said through the screen, "I don't think I can stand it. Such birds preyed on the bodies in our village when I was a child...."

"I'll blast them away," he said, his own boy voice an excited tremolo.

"I know you have to do your work," she said.

"Yes," he said, turning to scan the trees, "there comes the fall and the time when deans demand a reckoning and editors tear your manuscripts in a wanton way...."

But she couldn't answer. She was deep in the house by then.

Mrs. Hammer stood on the back step watching him, her heavy arms folded over one another. "Brrrr!" she said. "It all gives me the chills. I've never seen them come into town like that. Gulls come, but not crows."

He didn't say anything.

"And that Indian—he's a spooky one too—a smart aleck, which they usually aren't. You'd think jobs around here were begging for people."

"They're pretty awful!" he mumbled, looking off into the trees.

And then realizing he had said the wrong thing—but it was too late.

Mrs. Hammer was opening the door for him, her face earnest and flushed and a little frightened. "Say," she said, "you don't think that Indian put a hex on her, do you?"

"I don't think they do things like that," he said. "It's just coincidence."

"Could be the smell," Mrs. Hammer said and then, embarrassed, added, "they smell, you know."

"I don't think so," he said and then he saw that Mrs. Hammer was both embarrassed and indignant because he was not quite agreeing with her or paying attention to her. What the hell were they really talking about anyway?

All that afternoon and evening he fretted the Ibsen article to make the style appropriately scholarly and dense (he tried to laugh at that) for PMLA. When he opened his window to catch the breeze off Lake Superior he could hear Professor von Fange's typewriter clattering away like a frantic pulse. He fell asleep about ten. And into no dreams.

When he awoke he was startled to discover that he had slept twelve hours. He eased his aching body out of bed and dressed and lit a cigarette and coughed. Bad habit, but the only way he could keep himself at a typewriter for seven or eight hours every day. Narcotize oneself. Suck fire. Ignite oneself to frail deeds. Keep smoking your flesh away until you are....

He waited; his heart beating.

"The heart is half a prophet"—a Yiddish proverb.

At precisely 10:30 he heard their cawing and wild derisive cries. He went downstairs. Mrs. Hammer was baking something and had Duluth radio on full blast and was disregarding him and the crows.

The crows—punctual as stars. Ministers of darkness lingering among the trees.

What did they want? For whom had they come?

He walked over to the garbage cans next to Mrs. Hammer's garage and lifted the lids off both cans with the handles on top of each. Whew! What a stench!

He stepped under the wheeling and cawing crows and banged the covers together. A few flew away.

"You black devils!" he cried and slammed the covers together again. The rest slipped off deep into the cedars.

He stood there and listened. No typewriter working. No time working. Reluctantly, he turned to look at the professor's back door. No one there behind the screen darkly.

Someone was standing silently behind him. He turned to see who it was. Mrs. Hammer—all powdered white with flour from her baking. Ghostly baker of bread.

"It's so quiet," she said.

"Yes," he said.

"She's dead, isn't she?" Mrs. Hammer said.

"I'll have to go and see for myself, I suppose," he said.

Cousin Frog

Each morning at five o'clock my cousin Henry Waag puts on a pair of slick green rubber hip boots and walks three blocks to the Superior Bait Shop where he has worked for many years. He is a stubby little man with hunched, rounded shoulders and short arms that curve inward as he walks. Although he is not more than forty, his face is very old. His eyes are glaucous, protuberant and sad; his mouth thin and wide. Naturally people in town call him Frog or Polly-Waag. Once, a local science teacher, who was fired for teaching evolution as Gospel truth, said Henry just hadn't evolved as far as most folks; but nobody takes stock of any evolution talk. Henry is just what he is. God and his parents did it. Still, some people say Henry heard that remark or heard about it. You never know for sure about those things and how they affect people.

The bait shop has a wet floor and sloshy big concrete tanks over which aerators hiss fine spray to keep the bait fresh and alive. As he works— especially when there are no customers in the place—Henry talks affectionately to fathead minnows and gold chubs. "There you go," and "It's as good as home," he says again and again as he pours bucketfuls of the wiggling bait into the tanks. For a long time Henry played music for them, but that was before his old radio fell into one of the tanks and burned fuses and things and electrocuted eighty dollars worth of sucker minnows. Henry wept that day and has never kept a radio there since.

In the bait shop there are always leopard frogs sitting or hopping listlessly at the bottom of one of the concrete tanks. Henry puts lake weeds in there every day, but he never says anything to the frogs and never recommends them for bait even though they are supposed to be good for largemouth bass and northern pike. It happens every day. A customer stands looking down into the tank. "How much are the frogs?" he asks.

Henry says, "Don't even look at them. Bass are getting smarter than to go after a frog being pulled through the lily pads. Take one of those Hawaiian Wigglers and pork rind if you really want some action."

"But I want natural bait," the customer says.

"A frog on a hook is not a *natural* bait," Henry says.

About that time Henry's boss, Ivan, hears—over the hissing of the aerators—the customer say, "What is this anyway? Those goddam frogs for sale or not?"

Over to the tank steps Ivan with the cardboard sign that says: "Bass Special: $2.50 Doz." Henry has put the sign behind the tank. Ivan takes the customer's little white frog cages—most carry them on their hips—reaches down and, with an echoic voice, asks, "How many?" Then he sticks them into the frog cage, hands the cage to Henry and says, "You take care of this customer. He's a helluva fisherman."

Henry takes the man's money, slams open the old brass cash register and mumbles, along with the change, "Keep 'em wet and don't drown 'em. They ain't fish. They got to breathe. They're more aware than you'd believe. They even got ears you can't see. They ain't minnows or pollywogs. They got feelin's even."

"Jesus!" one of the customers will sometimes exclaim. "They relatives of yours or something?"

"Thank you," Henry says. Then he walks away and goes and squats down on the floor and broods.

Henry's boss has been thinking of firing Henry for years. But Henry is his brother-in-law and is, in fact, related to practically everybody in town. Firing Henry would bring on a civil war in the family even though nobody ever pays any attention to him or invites him anywhere. Besides, Henry works for minimum wage and has never asked for a raise or fringe benefits.

Still, Ivan watches every move that Henry makes—especially early in the morning when bass fishermen come in and when Ivan has his usual three chocolate doughnuts and a coke. "I'm keeping a journal on you," he says between swigs of pop. "I'm keeping track of things. I'm goin' to keep you hoppin'!" he says, smiling down at Henry.

But Henry is an aqueous and competent bait shop man. He can swish up a little netful of writhing crappie minnows and get exactly two dozen for tourist fishermen or the usual thirty-six for locals. And he can separate small, medium and large leeches into little white cups so fast they never have a chance to stick to his fingers.

There is one thing to fault though. Henry never *looks* at anyone. "Are these the right size hooks?" somebody may ask, or "Do you hook leeches through the head or tail?" and Henry may say "Yes" and "Either" as he stands there looking at hook or leech, but never looks at any*body*. A conversation with Henry is a conversation with a voice and a crumpled camouflage hat.

Most people in town are used to that and just say the old things like "That's Henry" or "A frog never really looks at you either so what do you expect?" But Henry makes outside people—people desperate for water and sun and the holy tug of a fish—nervous, and they complain to Ivan again and again. Sometimes they say, "Your man don't look at you, does he?" or "That fellow won't sell me the bait I want." Then Ivan says, "He's good with bait," or, if Henry has pretended to not *see* or hear someone, Ivan says, "He's a relative," and then the customer usually laughs.

The worst was the one time Henry was on jury duty. When the county attorney asked a witness, "Is that person in the courtroom?" and then, "Can you point her out for us?" and the witness pointed to Candace Jensen, everybody's eyes shifted and fixed on Candace. But not Henry's. His were narrowed yellow slits fixed on nothing. "Alert the jurors!" the judge snapped and Henry sat up, but even then he didn't look at Candace.

Ivan made Henry go to the optometrist one winter morning after Henry said he couldn't read the cash register. At coffee that day—after the examination—Dr. Natty shook his head and said, "He wouldn't look in my eyes" and everybody at the counter knew exactly who he was talking about.

"Old Polly-Waag!" somebody exclaimed. "He don't look at nobody!"

"He *ain't* anybody!" somebody else said. "He's somebody else than who he is. I couldn't know him anymore than I could know a voice on the radio without no name for it."

Then the conversation picked up. "Well, poor fellow, he never goes anyplace," Natty said, "so he's lost visual communication with people. The eccentricity of the old bachelor."

"The old what? Well, he's got to be going somewhere in that white suit," someone said. "He gets it cleaned every two weeks."

"And another thing," someone else said. "Them kids at school—they was supposed to draw moons in Mrs. Sundbeck's class and you know what?"

"No sir, I don't," someone said.

"Them kids put old Henry's face on their moons—the whole bunch except the Knutson kid, of course."

"I heard he can swim clear out to the Hayes buoy at night," someone said.

"Oh, come now!" Natty said. "That's five miles."

"Maybe. But another thing. Where does he disappear to?"

"Disappear to?" Natty really perked up then and looked like he might write something down on a napkin or something but he doesn't ever do that.

"How can you disappear without a car or bus or ambulance or hearse or anything else? He hardly ever uses that rusted out old Ford. So how do you account for it?"

"Damned if I know!" someone exclaimed.

"Hmmm," said Natty. "What we have here is a man of mystery."

Henry never goes to the Band Box Coffee Shop or to any restaurant. He buys groceries in Duluth—taking his old Ford to get them. What does he buy? Who knows?

Every evening at nine o'clock Henry closes up the bait shop and walks back to his apartment over the theater. Once in a while people—his own sister once—try to get him to stop and talk because his eyes are so sad, but he just mumbles and puts his head down and keeps walking, muttering, "I've got to get up there and join the show." When his sister tried to take his arm and hold him he hopped off the curb and knocked her away and just went on to his apartment. Later she told Ivan, her husband, "My brother's going crazy. How can he go to a show? He doesn't have a TV; he doesn't go to the movies."

"Why don't you ask him? He's *your* brother!" Ivan said.

"You can't talk to him," she said.

"Tell me about it," he said. "I'm keepin' track."

The stairway entrance to Henry's apartment over the Bijou is next to the lighted case where the movie posters are pinned up. He pauses for a moment. Sometimes people are standing in line to get tickets. Kids yell, "Hi, Polly!" and he waves back. "Going to your pad? It's a big jump from here!" some kid cries and then they all laugh. Henry never looks at the posters; he disregards them—even the alluring faces of the actresses. The show begins soon. The popcorn is sputtering in the lobby. Someone is saying, "Two, please." Henry just hurries.

Once Henry is in his apartment it's always the same ritual. How do we know this? Well, someone spied once. It's not a thing to be proud of, but Henry's sister was worried to death. Anyway, once he gets into his apartment he hops around, kicking off the hip boots and sometimes falling down when he trips on them. Then he slips out of the army surplus overall and tosses the crumpled camouflage hat on the floor. His underwear comes off next—army surplus O.D. things too.

He does not put the lights on, but a little light from the street filters through the glass block curving around one corner of the theater. A white linen suit hangs on a walnut valet in the middle of the wood floor; under it a pink shirt. He finds the underwear too—white silk things he slips into luxuriously. Then he puts the shirt on, standing there like a frog prince with his white legs sticking out from under the shirttail. The suit fits perfectly; the tie appears in a perfect knot. Oh, and the white shoes—special ones from Italy—they make him taller.

There are only two things in the room—the valet and a white director's chair with a blue canvas bottom and back. On the back of the chair he has written and crossed off words with white chalk—Author, Lover, Director. He has put Director back after crossing it out once.

He sits in the director's chair, his thin wide mouth happy and perhaps a bit smug.

He just sits there awhile. And then, of course, there is sound in the room because the show has started. He just sits there in that white suit and smiles. Oh, now, that's not right, come to think of it. He makes his mouth move like a mimic. Then I guess he's supposed to have said, "Higher! Higher!" But I don't know. We're a little ashamed of the spying. But then he was spying in a way too.

I keep on talking about Henry as if he's just doing the same thing day after day like he had for many years. Well, maybe that's the way we wanted it—things in their places—the peaceful feeling you get when you say, "There goes so-and-so to his or her place as usual."

But the thing is the theater closed. People stopped going to the show. They bought VCR's and sat at home.

Nobody knows what Henry did the first night he went up there into his place and probably went through all that business of putting on the white suit, etc. His boss and brother-in-law Ivan Hofsted didn't even think of warning Henry that the theater was closing. That would give us all away. It seems like when Henry came to work the next day everything went crazy. When Ivan came in to eat his doughnuts and drink his coke and kind of get used to the idea of working all day with Henry, he didn't see Henry around at all. Still, the shop was unlocked and the lights were on.

It was a customer who found Henry—a fellow from Minneapolis who comes up early in September to get in some late bass fishing. This fellow walked into the shop and then over to the frog tank. Ivan says when he got to the tank, he jumped back about a foot and yelled out scared.

"Who's that in there?" he yelled over at Ivan.

Well, it was Henry and Henry was sitting in one corner of it saying "Lord" or "Lower" or something. He was wet from the spray and shivering.

"You come out of there!" Ivan cried, but Henry wouldn't move.

The customer left, shaking his head and saying, "This is too much. Why the hell do you keep him around anyway?"

Ivan finally got Henry out of there by turning everything off and just pulling him out with the help of a couple of other men from the Square Deal Cafe.

Then Henry disappeared. They thought he'd maybe sit for a little while and drink the hot coffee they brought, but it was like he was something else not like Henry or even a man. It was like he was one of those creatures you see in a science fiction movie or something. They couldn't hardly touch him he felt so cold and strange and he just made funny noises and walked right through them, limping in a hobbly way from sitting so long in the cold tank—just limping out past the dock, past the boats and everything and into the Omsrud Swamp.

"Where you goin'?" the men called after him, but it was like he had no ears.

Then suddenly he said, "Oh, I'll be back when there's a show again."

He disappeared and it was a bad thing. Ivan and Henry's sister nearly got a divorce over the whole thing. "What did you do to my brother?"— she must've asked him that question a million times and all he could say was, "I don't know. I just don't know." There were some jokes about Henry too. "Old Henry's out splashing with the rest of them"—that was a one-liner.

But here's the thing. A frog is a natural creature. So what is Henry? Why couldn't the sheriffs from two counties and practically the whole town find him? And they never did.

A frog is a natural thing, but there are times when we're not so sure.

Sarah Cleaton lived out there by Omsrud Swamp and is a tall, strong woman with two big children. She says Henry hopped into her bed one night a couple of weeks after he disappeared and that he forced her. She wasn't sure what he forced her to. One afternoon after a terrible rain—a hundred-year rain—maybe eight inches—there were hundreds of little frogs out in the cemetery next to the church on Lake Kyle. And those kids in school—why they can't draw a moon or cut a paper one without asking the teachers, "Is there a frog on the moon?" The smart ones ask, "How did it get there?"

In the spring a young unmarried couple from St. Paul came up—hippie types trying for the simple life—you know the kind—and tried to start up the theater again. They worked hard at making the place look good— painting away and getting the curtains inside cleaned and so forth. They lived there too—in Henry's old rooms.

The first night there were maybe thirty people in the theater—kids mostly. The young woman was so upset when she saw how empty the theater was that they say she started crying and ran upstairs to their room.

It was there—just as the movie started—that she saw something sitting in a chair in the darkness—something that frightened her so much she fainted. She couldn't really describe it at all. "Was it white? Green?" She couldn't say. It was gone when she came to. The two of them left town in a couple of days. The young man was a Vietnam veteran and he was mad. He accused some people here of trying to scare them out of town after they'd bought a lot of things and tried to have a business.

What could we say, really? Sure, we knew who or what it was. But it's embarrassing. He's a relative to a lot of us. What can we say, really? Try to explain this kind of thing. He's just around someplace. It's a funny feeling, but we've got to live with it somehow.

HOLLEY
FUNERAL HOME

HOLLEY FURNITURE
STORE.

WALTON

The Romantic Undertaker

Dr. Liv leaned back wearily in his own blue dental chair and tried to doze off so he would not be sleepy during the funeral service that afternoon. Sometimes when he became very sleepy at a funeral he would nod off and his head and neck would suddenly go slack. Then he would jerk his head back and people would turn to stare at him and he would be very embarrassed. If anyone kidded him about it later—and they usually did—he would say, "Why, I guess I plan to sleep at my own funeral too, so why all the fuss?"

As a matter of fact, Liv was getting tired of funerals. The whole town was one large geriatrics ward. My God! He was fifty-five and a kind of flaming youth compared to the ancient widows and widowers living (and dying) there. In some ways it depressed him terribly. Dentistry—the maintenance of decaying teeth, etc., was always a losing, foredoomed proposition. Perhaps that's why dentists so often committed suicide. And then, week-on-week, he saw his own best work...ugh! Better not dwell on that one. Bury it. Ugh!

The phone rang. Liv groaned, heaved himself up from the chair and answered it.

"Hello."

"Hello."

"Who's calling?"

"You don't know? It's me—Olaf Holley."

"Well, sure," Liv said, "—who else."

"Can you come over for a while?"

"What for?"

"I can't say just now, but come anyway. You don't have any patients anyway."

"How do you know?"

"Oh, I have my ways."

So he had his ways and Liv had no luck trying to sleep so he might as well go to see "Holy Ole," as they called him, over at the Holley Furniture Store, in the back of which (it was a two-faced building with fronts on two parallel streets) was the Holley Funeral Home (Since 1947). The furniture store had a front just like the Our Own Hardware store except that it was painted blue. The funeral parlor had been a bowling alley years back. It had a cement block front painted white except for the Palladian doors Holley had painted ochre so they resembled a glass-paned, eternal sunrise.

"Yes, sir," somebody in town once said to Liv, "you see, he's got baby cribs on one side and caskets on the other. No wonder he drives two Cadillacs. He's got us coming and going."

"I never thought of that," Liv said, wishing he hadn't *ever* thought about it.

So down Main Street Liv went, striding along as he always did with great bounding steps as if he thought with each step he was going to hop or jump but was restraining himself. Of course, when he was drunk he didn't bother to restrain himself. He simply strode along like a large jackrabbit which had decided to walk, not run.

"Where you headed, Doc?"

It was Klefsaas, the operator of the Mobil station, the town's practical joker and teller of bad jokes. He stood in front of a grease pit over which a bulbous brown car hunched, spewing black oil into a drain funnel like a humped creature going morosely to the toilet.

"Holley's," Liv said, thinking what the hell business is it of yours anyway?

"Which one?"

Liv shook his head in disbelief. Ah, but the Mayor can't be rude. Liv stepped over toward Klefsaas and leaned into a gas pump. A mistake no doubt. He, Liv, would have to endure at least one bad joke. Death, taxes, bad jokes—all inevitable.

"He didn't say."

"Well..." said Klefsaas, stepping closer, his troll eyes dancing in his little round face under the visored cap.

"Yes?"

"He's just about the last person to let a fella down in this world."
Liv smiled a brittle smile and turned to go. But no use.

"Has the Mayor heard about the suits?"

Liv turned back to look hard at Klefsaas. He was smirking his thin
mouth and wiping his hands on a blackening towel, which, when he hung
it down from his belt, said "Property of Hotel Duluth" on the bottom
of it in purple letters.

"Suits? What suits?"

"The business with the blue serge suit."

"Oh, that kind of suit?"

"Well, for God's sake, what other kind of suit is there except suit suits?"

"Of course," Liv said.

Klefsaas was looking up and down the street and leaning closer to
Liv. It was going to be a really dirty joke for sure—something perverted
no doubt. Making love to cows? Necrophilia?

"You see," Klefsaas said, "when Mrs. Oren's husband died and Ole
had him all laid out, you know what happened?"

"I have no idea," Liv said.

"She turns to Ole and says, 'Oh, I just always wanted him to be buried
in a blue serge suit. It would go so nice with his hair and everything,
but there's no money for that too.'"

"Yes?"

"'Well,' says Ole, 'I got a fellow found yesterday morning passed on
down by the tracks laid out in parlor two. The county bought him a suit—a
blue serge by coincidence.'"

"Oh?" Liv looked at his watch, but no use.

"Well," said Klefsaas, "he showed her the other one and she nearly
started bawling. 'It's so nice,' she said, 'but I have to go now to get
groceries. All our relatives will be here tomorrow and they like to eat
tons of steak and potatoes. Funerals always rile up their appetites.'"

"She left then?" Liv asked. The car over the grease pit seemed to be
staring back at Liv as he looked over at its sad headlights. It, too, had
to endure the man fumbling around at it.

"I'll get to that. Sure she went, but she felt bad and swung her old
Buick around and come back in five minutes or so."

"Five minutes."

"Sure, and you know what she found?"

"No."

"There was her husband in a blue serge suit."

"My gosh," said Liv.

"Just then Ole come in and was beaming all over. 'Oh!' cries Mrs. Oren, 'my husband looks just wonderful, but how in the world did you do it so fast?' And you know what Ole said?"

"No," said Liv.

Klefsaas held Liv's arm. He was bursting with it all and he looked up the street toward Holley's with gleeful mischief, pressing his frog lips tightly together and holding his face with one greasy hand.

"He said, 'I just switched heads!'" Klefsaas said, choking and pressing the towel at his face.

"Thank you," said Liv, pulling his arm away. "Some joke," he said.

"I knew you'd like it, Doc," Klefsaas said between spasms of laughter.

Liv hurried to get to Holley's, cutting across the street in front of the only car in sight and barely dodging it. Behind him Klefsaas was still chuckling at his own joke, his face buried in the towel.

Liv stepped into the furniture store—one of two in town. He always preferred to enter there through the beds and end tables and carpet samples—and the baby cribs, of course. Not many were being sold. The whole place was neat and clean and silent as if all the people who used the furniture had departed—"Departed." Liv shrugged his shoulders at the word.

"Dr. Liv, I presume. How infinite in faculties...."

It was Ole Holley standing there at the corner of a huge oak bed, the post knobs for which were as large as bowling balls.

"This is a special order," he said, nodding toward the bed. "It is in bad taste. They are going to drill finger holes in these and maybe paint them black. They are both nuts about bowling. In fact, they are both nuts, you might say, but they have money now so they are opulently nuts."

Liv had to laugh, and while he was at it, laughed at Holley's appearance too. He was a strikingly handsome and dignified seventy year old man—tall, slim and straight. He looked like a statesman with his black silk suit and fine moustache and clear blue eyes. He conducted funerals with precision and dignity and great tact. Morticians know the ultimate intimacy, Liv mused—intimacies beyond those of bride and groom, doctor and patient. And so.... Yes, he was an impeccable gentleman—a would-be actor when he first went to the University—and then a—a mortician for some reason he had not yet shared with Liv. Perhaps he preferred being a director—if only a funeral director. Ha, ha! Liv laughed within himself at his own joke.

"Well," said Holley, "what do you think?"

"The epitome of bad taste," Liv said.

"The what?" Holley was turning—bending down to look into the mirror on the dresser that belonged to the bowling ball bedroom set.

My God! Liv saw that Holley was wearing a toupee. He turned to look at Liv again, his eyes pleading for approval of such daring.

"No, no," he said to Liv, "it can't be that. Besides, it's a gift."

"I meant the *furniture*," Liv said. "I didn't even notice the toupee at first. It...it seemed so natural."

"Really?" Holley said, turning to look into the mirror again, lowering his shoulders to keep the top of his head level.

"Yes, I mean it."

Holley was smiling then—his smile that comforted—the one he used most often during casket selection, Liv recalled. Be generous, it advised.

"It was a beautiful gift," Holley said again, his hands folded together.

"From whom?"

"Come along and you'll see."

Liv found himself being led into the other half of Holley's business— the mortuary. Plaintive German 18th century organ music was playing softly through invisible speakers as they walked on deep carpets toward (and Liv gasped, thinking about Klefsaas' joke) room number two.

"Here," said Holley, "is my dear benefactor."

Liv gasped again at what he saw. It was Grace Thorson, a patient—a former patient—from the Luther Memorial Home. It *was* her. Her body lay in studied and silent and waxed and delicately-rouged repose, her hands folded the usual way, her short gray hair stiffly sculptured, her head tilted slightly back.

"Doesn't she look like she is waiting for someone?" Holley asked.

"Well..." Liv began, "she looks...nice."

"All of them are beautiful," Holley said, his face set with the zeal of his words, his eyes bright and on the verge of tears.

"Hmmm," said Liv, recalling the rumor that Holley wore black silk suits *all* the time—even during that time when he worked on...them.

"Touch this," Holley said, bending over to let Liv touch the fine white hair of the toupee on top of his head.

"Hmmm," said Liv.

"I don't wish to be crass," Holley said, "but I, I had it done in Minneapolis—flew down there and back on the same day."

"Tuesday," Liv said.

"Yes, and I'm so pleased. It's comfortable too these cool days and it's a kind of blessing on my head—her blessing. She played piano. Lovely hands."

"Hmmm," said Liv.

"It won't be long now," Holley said.

"What?"

"The service begins in two hours. You'll be attending?"

"Always," said Liv.

"Well, forgive me, but I have to make a lot of arrangements so I'll have to be going." He paused. "You don't think I'm silly, do you? I hadn't thought of such a thing until she—she offered it. She had a kind of a sense of humor. She and I kidded about it. I'm rather severe and formal. It was good to kid. You have your other side, you know, so forgive me if I'm romantic or something in a crazy way."

"What's to forgive?" Liv asked, avoiding the casket with his eyes because he could swear there was a smile lurking *there* somewhere.

"Well," said Holley, shaking Liv's hand solemnly, "...until the service—the farewell, the auf Wiedersehn."

"Until," said Liv.

Liv stepped gingerly through the funeral parlor and the furniture store and out into the street. It was getting warm—very warm—out in the sun. When someone opened and closed the front door of the Square Deal Cafe a breath of sour beer and deep fryer grease huffed out at Liv and he hurried back to his office to do some odd chores and, he hoped, to rest a bit.

The funeral service was like all the others he attended at the Lutheran Church. Holley handled things with panache and great dignity. The hearse (the old wax-slick death buggy) was spotlessly elegant and patient at the curb. Of course, first there was a quick show of the departed, the other old ones leaning toward it to see—whatever they saw. It was all a blank to Liv, a waxen blank. Eyes closed. Nothing there.

He sat quietly in the back row to get as far away from the smells as he could. The primary odor was rank-sweet, rich with the perfume of fresh flowers, but soon other odors began to come up out of the huge furnace grate on the floor between nave and chancel—to come up from regions of cooking in the church basement: coffee fumes, oily and hot; the unctuous aroma of cold meat sandwiches and hot dishes; the rich, sweet smell of cake and frosting.

Oh, death where is thy frosting? No. Another bad joke, Liv mused.

Liv could visualize them down there in the basement—the women of the Ladies Aid pushing giant blue-black porcelain coffee pots over the yellow-blue flames of the gas burners; the steaming sinks; the great, fat red arms in the frothing dishwater.... He could see them because he had seen them *once* and that was enough. He always skipped the funeral feast after that.

"Pssst!" It was Holley, standing there to Liv's left. He had closed the church doors with miraculous silence after everyone was in.

The choir was shrieking an old Norwegian hymn. "I shall be raised up...to join the great white host...." the old voices cried.

"Barbaric!" Holley whispered, leaning over Liv's shoulder.

"What?"

"The smells...."

Liv nodded, hoping none of the others heard. He noticed Holley's face was beaded with sweat. Toupee. Improper cooling.

Holley stepped back and stood waiting. He looked terribly dignified standing there.

Suddenly the toupee closed itself up on the top of Holley's head like a giant upside-down tan mushroom. Then it poised there on the pink bald dome, rocking ever so slightly.

Holley felt it immediately, scooped it off into his suit pocket and slipped noiselessly through the church door. Liv got up, went out, stood at the top of the front steps and watched him.

Holley flew down the front steps of the church with four long stiff steps, dashed down the sidewalk to his funeral director's car, tugged open the door and glove compartment and put another toupee on his head. Liv slipped back into church and sagged into his seat. It had all taken only seconds. The Quick and the Dead.

They were ending the hymn and the pastor was mounting the pulpit. In that moment Holley stood next to Liv sitting there at the end of the pew. Liv looked up at him. He was perfectly calm, an elegant gentleman imperially fine and slim and handsome—especially his hair—his fine head of white hair, and he wasn't even out of breath. A man in control of his passions.

"This is my spare," he whispered to Liv.

"Hmmm," said Liv.

"She was always a little unpredictable, Grace was. Always kept you waiting too. Maybe a little too proud in some ways."

"I'll say," said Liv as Holley slipped through the yellow oak doors and went out to wait, like a patient gentleman caller, to take a lady for a ride in the country.

Mrs. Swenson's Patrol

The streets of the town had been blocked off from Highway 61 and the tourist cars by long sawhorses festooned with red, white and blue streamers. Above the center of Main Street a huge banner reading CHIPPEWA DAYS—July 15-16 tugged on ropes fastened to the fronts of the Blue Water Cafe and Nina's Boutique. In the brisk wind off the lake the banner ballooned out like a wide white sail.

And so did Mrs. Swenson's blue and white flowered dress as she led her daughter down the center of the street. She was a rotund woman with a glistening fat face and eyes receding behind her cheeks. When gusts of wind flapped her dress she stumbled a little and held the dress against her short thighs.

Her daughter—a thin girl in heels and jeans and a jean jacket—was turning smiles off and on as she walked in line after Mrs. Swenson. When Mrs. Swenson strode forward, her head turning from side to side as she surveyed the nearly empty streets, the girl grinned a brown little mouth and wiggled her head side-to-side in mimicky fashion. When Mrs. Swenson turned and looked—Buddhalike—at her daughter—the girl was solemn and attentive and even stopped chewing an enormous wad of strawberry bubble gum.

"I've got to change!" Mrs. Swenson cried once in a while. "It's too windy for a dress."

"Oh, Ma!"

"You never mind. You just be glad we can get in here and get groceries before they come."

"Oh, Ma!"

"You stop that 'Oh, Ma!' or you'll get yours," Mrs. Swenson said without turning to look at her daughter. "And stop gawking at those gulls. They are hideous creatures. They would eat your flesh if they could."

She walked forward, her bosom tight and extended, her flats flap-flapping quietly on the asphalt pavement.

"Bananas, wieners, butter—is that all?" she asked.

"Ice cream!"

"Amy, it don't keep hard in the old fridge, so skip the ice cream. I could use some celery to chew on. They say you use up more calories chewin' it than you take in. There's no grace for a chunky woman these days."

"Why can't I get what I want?"

Mrs. Swenson turned around then, her bosom looming over the wiry body of her daughter. "You been listening to your father on the phone, haven't you. Well, he's a sucker for your little tears and such, but I have to make ends meet up here while he's having the good life down there."

"Why did we come here?"

"Because I went to high school here. Say, why am I tellin' you this for the hundredth time anyway? You aren't retarded, are you?"

Amy did a little wobbly jerk with her head, rolled her eyes widely and said, "Why not? My parents were cousins."

"You better stop the cute stuff and get serious. There is danger in the air...."

"Those are gulls," Amy said, looking up at a gray gull pivoting overhead. She squinted into the sun just before her mother's pink hand slapped the side of her head.

"Ow!" she cried, "—owie, owie!"

"That's nothing compared to what *could* happen to you," Mrs. Swenson said.

"You don't have to slap."

"Oh, yes, I do."

They were approaching the IGA when they heard it—drums somewhere.

"Jesus Lord! We've got to hurry!" Mrs. Swenson exclaimed. "We could get caught on the streets. It starts at noon."

"Oh, Ma!"

"Shut up. There are things you don't know...." They were inside the store and Mrs. Swenson began tugging angrily at a cart that would not disengage from the others. When it came loose she lurched backward and knocked a display of Cheerios (Special $1.49) down.

"Now look what you've done!" Amy cried.

"*I* did? A cart sticks like that so I practically pull a muscle and then it's my fault. I could almost sue them. My fault, baloney!"

A quick boy with a black bow tie and a white shirt and apron came over, smiled at Amy and began putting the display up again as Mrs. Swenson, reciting her grocery list, angrily pushed the little special tray down inside the cart.

"Hi!" the boy said to Amy.

"Hi!"

"You come along now!" Mrs. Swenson snapped.

As they walked down the store aisles, Amy ran like a little bird back and forth to the items. "You think you're cute, don't you!" her mother called after her. "You think you can just smile that teeny face of yours and wiggle that body and get what you want, but you wait and see."

"Please, Ma!"

"Don't 'please Ma' me. You're going to get into trouble doing that someday."

"Same as you?"

Mrs. Swenson swung her body around the cart and caught her daughter with one hand and slapped her behind with another. With an indignant cry Amy ran out of the store.

"You little snot! You little snot!" Mrs. Swenson mumbled to herself. Behind her, an older couple with a cart full of macaroni and cheese lunches backed their cart away and slipped down another aisle.

You think because you're cute you can do what you please, don't you, Mrs. Swenson said to herself. She was nearly crying, her eyes brimming with tears, her body lurching against the cart while she tried to focus on per-unit prices on the shelves.

At the check-out counter she bought a copy of the *National Enquirer*. "I've always loved Desi Arnaz," she said to the check-out girl. "Now they say he's dying of cancer."

She came up fifty-six cents short.

"You take the frozen peas back," she said. "Kids don't need so much vegetables in the summer."

Outside, the drums were getting louder, rattling against the wind itself and she cried out as she saw nobody was in the parking lot as she stood there with the sack of groceries in her arms.

But then there was Amy peeking around the corner. Mrs. Swenson stopped sniffling. "Damn you!" she said. "You don't care, do you? You just let me walk around alone scared half to death while those Indians are coming."

Amy took the sack, carrying it with both hands. Then they began the trek back to their trailer house perched above the town behind the county garage. Amy followed her mother closely. Mrs. Swenson wasn't talking; she did not talk for days sometimes if Amy did things—especially if Amy was invited to parties or was babysitting in nice homes.

Drum rhythms rattled against the walls of the county garage as they approached it, Mrs. Swenson panting from the climb.

"Lord God!" Mrs. Swenson cried. "They're upon us!"

And a high school band marched across their path, the drum major strutting with his head thrown back, his tall gold-braided hat staying miraculously on. The band—in purple and gold uniforms—passed by, eyes fixed forward, their instruments flashing gold and silver in the morning light.

"It's Odin High!" Amy exclaimed. "That guy is Orton Hanson!"

"He looks silly!" Mrs. Swenson said. "He looks like he may fall backwards on his you-know-what!"

"Oh, Ma!"

"And listen. It could've been them—the Indians. The drums do different things to them—wild things."

"Oh, Ma!"

"You shut up!" Mrs. Swenson stood watching the band move with regular steps down past the public library and the hospital. She was breathing heavily and sweat shone on her forehead.

"They'll wake them up, for God's sake!" she said. "Those old people in the hospital will all be woken up. Those young people don't care about anybody."

"Ma, it's 11:00 in the morning."

"They sleep late," she said. "They are old and tired."

The house trailer was parked on a ledge cut by a caterpillar tractor on the side of a hill. Mrs. Swenson rented the trailer for $250 a month. Her old Mercury was parked at one end of it, its headlights staring up from the incline. Mrs. Swenson was afraid to drive it and always had a neighbor man park it and back it down to a level street.

Inside the trailer Mrs. Swenson plopped down on a bench in the kitchenette while Amy put the groceries away. When she was done, Amy sat looking at the *Enquirer* and popping her bubble gum.

Mrs. Swenson ripped the paper away. "You don't read such things!" she cried. "This is for adults."

"It's silly anyway!" Amy cried.

"I'm keeping current. I don't want to be a know-nothing."

"Can I go downtown?"

"My God, what does it take to get through to you? The Indians are coming into town."

"I've seen them at school. They're neat...."

When she replied, Mrs. Swenson's voice was sharp-edged with irony. "Sure," she said, "they're neat. That's all you expect, isn't it? They just have to be neat. Well, you just listen to me. They are loose—very loose—and they get liquor and then the men go crazy—especially for the whites—you know...the white girls."

"The whites?" Amy was alert and attentive, her eyes focused seriously. But then she laughed. "Oh, it's not like that at all."

"'It's not like that?' You guarantee that? You always say, 'Oh, we won't this or that,' but then you had the motorcycle accident you *guaranteed* wouldn't happen. You can't control some things...."

"Maybe not, but they seemed kind."

"God, you're naive. They *seemed*. Things are not what they seem."

"I could go with Julie."

"So it could happen to two of you."

"What could?"

"An attack. They can trap you—no witnesses or anything."

"Oh, Mother, oh, that's crazy."

"No, you listen to me. They *get* crazy; then it's crazy. So I'm laying this rule down. You do not go downtown without me or your father."

"My father?" Amy sat back in her chair, her whole body stiffening, retreating into the cushions.

"He's maybe coming up tonight."

"How do you know?"

"He called."

"Is he going to stay here?" She pulled her ankles tight against her seat.

"Can he afford a motel? If he has to go to a motel he won't have that money to give us. Then what?"

"Can I stay overnight at Julie's? We'll stay at home. You can check with her mother."

"Mrs. What's-her-name? I wouldn't check with her about anything.

She's not a responsible person after the accident."

"Please?"

"Don't nag. I won't take it."

"I've got to go to Julie's. It's important."

"Don't you see what you're doing to me?"

"What?"

Mrs. Swenson shook her head in disbelief. "Oh, you are wearing me out so I can't stand it."

"Does that mean you're going to drink?"

Mrs. Swenson swung at Amy's face but missed. As she sat back on the bench her face became severe and tight.

"That means no talk now, doesn't it?" Amy said into the silence in the trailer.

Mrs. Swenson didn't reply. Then she began reading the *Enquirer* and chewing noisily on celery sticks pulled off a green stalk.

Amy turned on the TV. From 12:00 until 3:00 she watched game shows mostly. From time to time drum beats and cries of Indian dances echoed up the hill from Main Street. At 3:00 she put on her bathing suit to lie in the sun, but after she had lain there by the car for a few minutes, she felt a chill deep inside her stomach.

She got up and dressed and sat looking out the window at the lake. The gulls swung freely over it. A tall-masted sailboat hung on the distant edge of the water and then disappeared. She looked around the side of the trailer. Her mother was there, but not really there. She was deep inside a copy of a Danielle Steel novel and she was sitting there breathing in a hulk of a body, but she was not really there.

There was nobody there, except herself—Amy's self.

At 9:00 the drums stopped and all Amy could hear was the beating of her own heart.

Her mother had been drinking a lot—wine coolers and beer. She stood up, her eyes out of focus, and lurched down the narrow hallway of the trailer and fell heavily into her bed and then snored.

He came about 10:30. He was very cheerful and quite drunk himself as he watched TV. He brought presents and gave her spending money and called her "Honey."

She tried to stay awake, but after a while her eyes simply closed and she slept in the chair.

He was doing things to her—her father.

She let her body go. She did not want it anymore. She made her brain go away. She made her thoughts gulls that floated white and pure over blue water. His beard was a cedar tree. Her thoughts were gulls far off the shore. She began to concentrate on one gull—a gull that stayed far out from the shore and the trees. Her body fell away from her and she began to fly into the infinite lands of the sun. After a while even the body of the gull fell away and it was just a white wing in oceans of space where nothing had a name.

The Last Turkey Shoot

To: The Ed of *Hunting, U.S.A.*
Re: The Last Turkey Shoot in our Town of Odin, U.S.A. Under the
Supervision of the Odin Sportsman Club

Dear Ed,

Yes, sir, it would've torn at your heart to see those bronze birds torking through the air for the last time out of that cat-a-pult while the crowd cheered.

Yes, sir, I said the *last* time and that is sad and that is why I'm writing to you. It even made a he-man like Jack Swanson cry. Jack is this broad-shouldered fella in our club who fights at inter-mission time at dances. He and some wiseguy go out behind the Blue Goose Ballroom and everybody turns their car lights on Jack and his opponent and they rip each other's silk shirts apart—things like that. Of course, I'm only jokin' about the cryin'. It was really the black powder out of his muzzle loader that did that. POOF! And the powder in the pan singed Jack's eyebrows and torched the hair right up inside his big honker of a nose so it looked like the burned barrels of an old double-barreled shotgun.

I can see I'm di-gressing so I better focus on the issue as they say. The question is not "What is a turkey shoot better than?" The question is "What is better than a red-blooded, All-American turkey shoot?" Well, let me tell you, nothing is. For one thing there is shooting, danger and suspense. Take danger (see above about Jack Swanson's nose and eyebrows). Of course, the turkeys probably thought it was dangerous too—until later. (See below. You'll see they probably could of cared less then). There is using our natural resources. And, of course, there is patriotism. The turkey would've been our national bird if it weren't for Thanksgiving which has no connection at all with the eagle, which is our national bird.

Then there is preparedness. The muzzle loaders we use are like those Ethan Allen used when he and the Green Mountain Boys crossed over a mountain and hay-rassed the Redcoats. And it teaches a man to be a good loser like the Democrats. Now, I don't mean to start trouble over politics. I know my politics agree with yours. I never met a hunter whose didn't. And I try to be fair. Even the President had to be a good loser in that film in which he lost the girl to Gabby Hayes, who was not wearing a beard or clicking his teeth way back then.

Speaking of trouble, it was partly the libbers that started the beginning of the end. How, you ask? Well, by telling us that in our turkey shoot we were terrifying women, children and dogs and had better use frozen or other already-dead birds or *else*.

Or else, what? you are probably thinking. A sex strike is what. You heard me right. That's what Emma Hildesheim, the postmaster's wife told him.

"A strike is communist," Henry told her and she says, real smart, "That's right. It's I.W.W.—the *I Won'ts of the World!*" Can you imagine?

Jack Swanson walks up to him at the P.O. window where he is picking up his copy of you guessed it—*Hunting, U.S.A.*—and Jack says to Henry, "If you got any last night, smile."

And Henry just looks grim and shakes his head and says, "It's the I.W.W."

"Well," says Jack, "you might say it's a new *zip* code."

Well, wait a minute. I have got to be fair. It was also Doc Liv, our mayor and dentist, that helped bring it about. It was at our next-to-the-last shoot and we had just crowned Miss Susan Iverson "Miss Turkey Shoot." (She was a good sport about her eyebrows being burned off, etc.) The barbecue was beginning and there was enough tuna-macaroni salad in that washtub in the Legion Club to feed Chicago and I had just shot an old tom right through the eye and Doc Liv comes over to me in the Legion and starts in like a prophet of doom.

"This can't go on forever," he says to me.

"Why," I says, "there's enough tuna-macaroni salad there for all the people in Two Harbors."

"The turkey shoot, I mean," he says.

"Oh?" I asks with some suspicion.

"Sooner or later someone is going to protest to the Society For the Prevention of Cruelty to Animals," he says, refusing with one hand some more of the salad which is always good. Jake Benson, the American Legion cook, makes it fresh.

"But a bird isn't no animal," I says.

"But it's one of God's creatures and is generally held to be responsible for Thanksgiving Day," he says.

"Well," I says, "that is a non-squirter if I ever heard one and I just did. You can't eat an eagle. And, besides, if God didn't want turkeys shot or otherwise he wouldn't have given us shotguns and them those big drumsticks or let women discover sage dressing."

Well, what could that dentist from Chicago say to that? I had him and he knew it. He stopped sneering at the salad and turned and saw how happy Miss Turkey Shoot was as she rode in the back of Jack Swanson's pickup waving at people and smiling and wearing that headdress with the bronze feathers in it and holding a congenial turkey under each arm. We gave her a $50 scholarship that year to UMD, but I heard she bought artificial eyebrows with it and is going to beauty school over in Superior, Wisconsin.

But the other women.

Say, they ought to realize that hunting is a sport.

But that Emma Hildesheim, the I.W.W. postmaster's wife (he wasn't— she was) had been eavesdropping while I talked to Doc Liv and she comes over (it took her about one step: she is six feet tall and mannish with her size, wears a size XL Mackinaw if you can imagine.) She stands there looming over me and says, "It's a *cruel* sport. You ever shoot a baseball or a football?"

Well, I looked right at her Mackinaw and I says, "No, but neither one of them has a drumstick. I suppose you could stuff a football with sage dressing and mashed potatoes, but it would be deflating for Thanksgiving."

Well, what could she say to that? She just says, "You men! You're cases of arrested development," which I disregarded because I have never got a traffic ticket—except—well, anyway....

These women just don't understand, do they? You think about it sometimes. We have got to be aggressive and take hold. Ten below and colder than a well digger's _____ in Alaska and a foot of snow on the ground and an old tomcat is out there yowlin' out his hot lament.

That, my friend, is the spirit that won the West, not some kind of womanish idealism.

But what's the use? The I.W.W. and a few other restless women got together with Doc Liv and brought the end. The terrible thing is that we were taken in by it because we was tryin' to be fair-minded. Taken in—not by the I.W.W. of course. Ha!

How, you ask?

Well, by makin' us use Firds. Firds is Frozen Birds all squashed into one word. Compressed is what they call it—the word. The birds are the same size but stiff and frosty like some women I know.

Now we are not against progress and social improvement, let me tell you. We used those Firds and tried to make the best of it. Let me tell you about it.

We had to get them first. It was easy. Hundreds of them was caught out in the Armistice Day blizzard (that was in November) and froze to death under the snow. We dug out a few stacks of them and put them into a big locker—a kind of unused natural resource.

Of course, while suffocating under that snow they pressed their wings close to their bodies (like this) to keep warm so they weren't *positioned* much for flyin' until maybe the Resurrection Day (we don't know what month that will be in.) So what does Doc Liv do? He gets this professor from UMD to help us make a cat-a-pult for $25. Actually it was just a big slingshot made out of tractor inner tubes and a DeSoto car frame.

I have to say that there was both good things and bad things about using frozen birds. It was a real challenge to shoot at a frozen turkey torking through the air. You never knew what one of them was going to spring on you. They were completely unpredictable. It depended on what position they was frozen in. Pre-destination I think the Presbyterian minister called it.

"Pull!" one of us would yell and that cat-a-pult slingshot would fire a Fird out with a huge tu-wang! and the DeSoto car frame would quiver all over after doing it like some people I know.

Did I say it was a challenge? Well let me tell you. Some went whipplin' sideways like bundles of shingles in a tornado. Some went straight up like rockets, their frozen purple legs stiffin' out behind. Oh, and some went cat-a-pulting end-over-end—hoot/wheet! hoot/wheet!—like that. You had to lead them just right to get the 4-chill shot into them and then the judges had a terrible time deciding if they was hit at all. "Look there!" one of them would say, "the shot is bouncin' off with hardly a twitch or a fallen feather." It gave you the chills, sometimes, I tell you—especially if you shot straight overhead and an icy feather fell down the neck of your hunting jacket. Once in a while one would whiz off and go through a car radiator or stick in the ground like a wood-carved ostrich. No live turkey would do that now, would it? It would be un-natural.

That was the FF (Flyin' Fird) Competition. Then there was the SSF (Simulated Sneaky Fird) Competition in which you put a turkey on the other side of a log with just its head showing.

This latter is why it all ended. There has to be some joy and dignity in a tradition or it doesn't amount to anything. Can you imagine? There you are with a .50 caliber muzzle loader that could give a grizzly bear the rigors of mortis. You snucker down on another log fifty yards away and take aim and there is a frozen little eye (they brush the snow off) beadin' at you over the log. Why, it froze your trigger finger and put a zero right in your own eye.

And another thing. You can't have a barbecue with birds that have died a natural death in a snowbank on Armistice Day in November. You have to shoot them or something *before* not *after*. They have got to bleed.

So that is why it all ended. That was the last turkey shoot in Odin, U.S.A. A lot of us sportsmen are sad about it. I believe that down in his heart old Doc Liv is too. All that shootin' used to jar fillings loose here and there not to mention the disastrous results of biting down hard on bird shot in a slice of dark or light meat at the barbecue between helpings of tuna-macaroni salad.

But things change, don't they?

We are desperately trying to fill the void as they say. We have a committee working on Cedar Stump Dynamiting. You sit in a big circle around the stump and drink Coors and wait for the thing to go torking up, et cetera. Doc Liv says it looks like a big black tooth jumping right out of somebody's jaw—somebody who chews tobacco.

But it's not the same—no powder burns, no hoo-loo-loo of those birds before they get shot.

We did the stump dynamiting in the spring. There's nothing else to hunt in the spring in Odin.

Dear Ed, we ask you—what can we sportsmen do to replace the loss of another great American tradition?

Your suggestions in this matter will be greatly appreciated if they are any good.

Yours in hunting and shooting as well as fishing, etc. Occasionally

I do go to a Cedar Stump Dynamiting, but see above.

Lester Flint, Pres.

Sportsman Club (And Tall Talers)

Odin, U.S.A.

P.S. I naturally hope your wife is
    no I.W.W. and that you are
    smilin' this very minute, if you
    know what I mean.

The Owl and the Mailbox

Irene and Hans Olson sat in the kitchen of their cabin on Devil's Track Lake drinking coffee and watching the snow settle in large, easy flakes on the cedars and aspens and the road behind the place. Hans was a wiry little man with flashing blue eyes and quick hands. A black, cast-iron range, over which his wife worked, snapped and popped merrily. She was humming something and making breakfast and it was warm and cozy in the kitchen; but Hans was not a happy man. He was reading a letter over and over, smoothing it out on the table and examining it in detail. From time to time he scowled down at the thing.

"They think they can pull this off," he said to Irene finally. "They think because I'm older now I won't fight 'em, but that postmaster dude isn't putting me off with a letter. He hasn't got the nerve to come himself. He's probably cowering behind his cage in there at the P.O. and thinking, 'That official letter will do the trick.' Those snowflakes out there—they mean they'll be sending the plow out after a bit."

Irene turned with a big blue skillet full of eggs and potatoes and sausage in one hand and ladled Hans' plate full.

"You sit now too," he said. "I'll do the dishes."

"Well, I don't know," she said, wiping her hands and sitting down. "It seems you might be too nervous to handle dishes." She was a tall, copper-haired woman with big shoulders and a long face and a pointed nose, red with the heat of the stove.

"Oh, sit down," he said, patting her seat fondly.

"I don't like it," she said, looking out at the snow. "You can't take on the government all by yourself. They'll have the FBI or something."

"Yes, I can," he said, after Irene finished grace for both of them.

"Good potatoes," he said. "Just the right amount of pepper."

"Not you," she said. "You got too much pepper in you. You could use a little more butter."

"Look who's talking. You lose ten more pounds fooling around with that TV diet and I'll think I'm sleeping with a snow fence."

"You talk like that you will," she said, handing him the butter. She was eating one egg and a piece of toast.

"The only government worth a damn is the Forest Service," he said, leaning an arm on the table and sipping his coffee. "They're the only ones know what they're doing. What does a postmaster in Odin who took a civil service exam know?"

"He knows he makes thirty-six thousand a year," Irene said.

"Oh, sure, and earns every damn cent sitting in there snooping in people's mail and then trying to threaten people."

"I doubt it."

"Doubt what?"

"He snoops."

"Well, well," he said. "Now we got the hots for Jim boy. Thirty-six thousand is it? So? The Don Juan of OHS he was!"

"That's crazy," she said. She was getting up, taking her plate and coffee cup with her. When they quarreled she sat at her little sewing table and ate, and then, if no peace was made by bedtime, she would sleep on the cot in the pantry.

"Oh, boy! Now I've done it," he said. "Whew! Now I've done it. I ain't really mad at you, you know." He walked over to the stove, picked up the porcelain coffee pot and walked over to pour her a refill. She took it. Sometimes she covered the cup with her hand if she was especially angry.

He stood there looking at her. In the little flashes of flame from around the edges of the stove door her copper hair shone richly and he touched it with one hand. "I just gray," he said, "but you got that copper hair that makes me feel rich."

She kissed his hand. He bent over and kissed her hair.

"It's snowing heavy now," she said, putting his hand on her shoulder.

"Ya, I see that."

"And the county plow'll be coming."

"I suppose so."

"You think they'll do it?"

"Sure. The Alquist kid sits with the driver. He's the one who roughed up Louise...."

"Before you roughed him up...."

"After he wasn't a damn bit sorry and had a sneer a yard wide on his big face...."

"That was fifteen years ago. He was probably scared."

"Good," he said. He walked over and watched the snow white-mossing the trees outside. There off to the right, a horned owl perched on a tall cedar. Its breast was mottled and streaked with white and gray. It was turning its head from side to side as if scanning the place.

"He's around too, I see."

She got up and walked over and stood by him. "I saw him too," she said. "He's a quiet one."

"The rabbit never hears a thing until the beak and claws and wings are there. Then it's red snow. Rabbit never has a chance."

"You're too serious," she said. "Maybe we should go and see that movie in Two Harbors—the one with Rodney What's-his-name—the comic."

"First I got to deal with this," he said.

"You don't want to just move it? It sure would be easier."

"Say, you sticking with me or not?" he said, turning away from the window to look at her, his face riven with a grief just then.

"I was just asking."

"Well, I'm not moving it."

She turned and touched her hair and looked in the mirror over the washstand. "I might go to Norman's," she said. "It's getting so long."

He watched the road. "That Norman is a pretty young thing," he said. "All the ladies get touched by him. Pay twenty-five dollars to get fondled a little."

"I don't," she said, "but you are a little stiff these days in bed—like hugging a...."

"...a snow fence?"

She smiled. "Not exactly."

"With a fine post...."

"Oh, ya. Fine."

"I'll get these dishes done," he said. "I have to have something useful to do."

"You worked twelve hours a day for forty-four years. Isn't that enough?"

"I thought it was, but I get restless."

"Ya, but don't try to take on the government, and let me wash this time."

She walked over, nudged him aside with her hip and started washing the plates.

"Oh, I got to," he said rinsing. The water was so hot it steamed the little kitchen window and he could not see the owl out there.

"I suppose it'll keep snowing," she said, "so I better get ready."

"If you want to...I figure as soon as the snow quits it'll be here."

"You couldn't move it a couple of feet, I suppose. That's all they want."

"No, I couldn't because then they'll want something else."

"What would that be?"

"You'll see."

She finished washing everything—dishes, the oilcloth on the table. Then she went over to the washstand and stood combing out her hair. Her long pale face was curtained on both sides by the long coils of it.

"That is where my father put that box," he said, standing by the front window. "That is where they put his citizenship papers. That is where my brother's draft notice came. I remember the day my father and I put it in. It's in solid rock...."

"I know all that," she said.

"Then why do I have to explain?"

"I'm worried," she said.

"Well I want to make *them* worry," he said. "The meek are always having to move things. They get pushed around. They inherit a little only when the others decide they might just allow it."

"That's not what I heard," she said. "That is not what we're supposed to believe."

Suddenly there was a burst of sunlight through the front window and the frolic architecture of the snow stood out glistening and beautiful in the light.

"Why a snowplow?" she asked. "What has a county plow got to do with the federal post office?"

"You know the government people," he said. "They're all conspiring together—the CIA and the whatever. The Forest Service never pulls that kind of monkey business."

She shook her head. "But it's the county who says the box is twenty-seven inches out on the road."

"Don't overcomplicate," he said. "They're in cahoots, you can bet on it."

"What difference does twenty-seven inches make?"

"On a winding road too," he said. He was smiling.

"A curvy one in thousands of trees."

"Whew!" he said. "Any time now. Like Hill 292 in Korea. They just come at you all at once."

He pulled on an olive green snowmobile suit and lifted his old Krag-Jorgensen rifle off its wooden pegs above the boots lined up next to the door.

"You mustn't shoot anyone," she said.

"A snowplow isn't anyone," he said.

"They could arrest you."

"They'll be trespassing. I have established my rights by two generations of adverse possession!" he said, flicking the bolt action back and forth.

"My! My! But I don't want to be left here alone," she said. She was putting on her own snowmobile suit and cap and heavy insulated boots.

He smiled. "By God, you're something," he said.

"But if you shoot somebody we're both nothing."

"I'm not so dumb," he said. "I won't do that."

Outside the cabin the snow was deep and powdery blue-white. They walked side by side, their tracks vague in the depth of it as they moved down the driveway.

The mailbox—a homemade wooden one—was mossed with snow too and looked humble enough. It stood on a little promontory of stones hidden under plowed and fresh snow that curved out suddenly from a long straight barricade left by the snowplow. The black letters on the side of it read Irene and Hans Olson. The two of them stood next to it—one on each side.

"They gave me crap at the cafe about the Irene too," he said patting the snow off it. "But I tell them my name comes first on every damn thing I get and I don't want that postmaster to fall asleep. Besides he's got the hots for you and this is sheer torment for him."

"Oh, that's silly!" she said.

Far down the road they heard the howling of an engine and the squeal of a steel blade on gravel and asphalt. Hans swung the rifle off his shoulder and cradled the barrel on his left arm.

They stood there waiting. She blinked her eyes and touched his arm. When she saw the look in his eyes, she pulled her hand back.

And then, suddenly, it was in sight, soaring down toward them like a giant bird of prey, snow churning off the two wing-blades of the plow, the faces of the driver and rider darkly outlined behind windshield wipers flapping at the flying powdered snow.

"He said to me—that County Road son-of-a-bitch, 'You been warned. You been discussed. Now the snowplow will take care of it because it is illegal.'"

They stood just behind the mailbox. The little red flag was up because Irene had mailed bills.

"Do you think they will see us?" she asked. "I'm afraid standing here."

"Oh, they see us all right," he said.

"Here it is!" she cried, tightening her scarf at her neck.

The big county plow rose up from a dip in the road two blocks away and flew down toward them, slowing down but not stopping.

Irene closed her eyes and held her breath.

The big wing bent away and passed no more than three feet away, exploding new snow against both of them, staggering them and leaving their ears and eyebrows full of it.

"Damn you!" Hans cried. He tilted the rifle up. Its barrel was clogged with snow and he tried to blow it out.

"Oh, don't!" Irene cried.

The plow stopped a block past them. The driver's door opened and a shrill voice cried, "You are crazy, you know. I got my orders to plow straight and sooner or later I'll get that thing out of there."

"Try it, you trespassing bastards!" Hans yelled. He did not lift the rifle off his arm again. Irene's mittened hand held the barrel.

The driver waved a contemptuous arm at them and drove off.

"Well," said Hans, shaking his shoulders and examining the muzzle of his rifle. "I got snow down my neck and a helluva chill. How about you?"

"Same here," she said.

"We better go in and take a bath," he said.

She shivered a little. "Ya!" she exclaimed.

Inside the cabin they heated water and took a bath together. It took them a long time to scrub each other nicely pink. Then they talked to each other and smiled. When they stood up and held each other, her copper hair dangled on his chest.

"What a mine it is!" he whispered, digging his fingers into the hair. "I feel rich and deep."

"You're not retired yet," she cried.

Then, before they slept, she lay next to him, her hand on him, and said, "You outlaw you and now I'm one too."

"We'll have to go out and do that when it snows. They won't give up so easy."

"That's nice," she said.

"Every time it snows," he said.

She yawned. "Excuse me," she said.

They were silent together. They heard sounds in the night they had not heard for a long time—timbers stretching a little, the popping of the stove.

"Even the cabin is excited," she said, yawning again.

And then the slow hooting of an owl.

"Him!" he said. "They're always around." He massaged her left shoulder where it ached sometimes. "Of course, they'll get it sooner or later. We aren't going to live forever."

"I feel lonely," she said.

"Me too," he said.

"I mean I'm not complaining," she said.

"I know."

He got up and went to the window and looked out into the silver moonlight on the woods and snow. For just a moment he saw a flicker of wings and then a shadow descending into the little meadow by the cedars.

"Ah!" he cried.

"Come on in here!" she cried.

He turned and ran and jumped into bed like a little boy.

In the morning it was snowing again and they both sat up in bed and watched it fall.

"Well?" he said finally.

"It comes again," she said.

She shivered and tried to cuddle him. "I feel lonely," she said.

After breakfast—a very late breakfast—they dressed and walked down to the mailbox. "Oh, let me put the flag up," she said. "It's a gay thing."

"We should fly the American flag the Legion gave me," he said. "By God, if I had a 3.5 bazooka I would fix 'em good."

"Oh, don't talk that way."

"The damn thing almost took us out."

"I know, but there are people in it," she said. She walked over and tipped up the little red flag. "Maybe they'll stop," she said.

"I doubt it," he said. "There's no one around and they could claim it was an accident."

A car approached—and another. It was a little convoy of two cars and a pickup.

"Who's that?" he asked.

"Millie and Peter," she said.

"Well, my gosh!"

The cars and pickup stopped, all lined up along the road. Each seemed to settle quickly into the snow. But the people were up and moving—some of them with picnic baskets.

"We've brought food!" a cheery face cried.

"It's reinforcements!" someone behind her yelled.

A woman with a cherry-red face was standing there patting the mailbox affectionately with a mittened hand.

"Millie!" Irene said, hugging her.

"We've got food," she said. "We're going to watch with you."

"Oh, my!" Irene cried. "But it's like a funeral or something...."

"Not on your life! It'll be their funeral. We'll stand out here and witness and drink coffee and eat sandwiches and cake. Maybe do a bit of our old cheerleader routine. *Give me an O!*"

"And I got akavit!" someone cried out behind her. "You can start a tractor at forty below with a thimbleful of it."

"I want to stop one, not start one," Hans said.

They all went into the house. There were eleven of them. They shook hands and nodded to one another. They were all retired people from along the road.

"I saw it happen!" Ernest Jensen said. He was a retired barber who always wore a baseball cap to cover his bald head.

"They think they can just use power any way they want...."

"It was that damn dentist governor who put that man in the P.O."

"Now let's not get political!" Millie cried. "Let's get the troops out of the house and to the outpost."

Outside, they all stood at a kind of attention, the coffee cups steaming in their hands.

When the plow came, it came slowly, then paused about a block away.

"Go ahead! Try it!" Ernest Jensen yelled, raising his mittened fist toward the plow.

But the driver and guide were out of the plow and walking toward them—two stocky young men in white coveralls—two snowmen. Behind them the great wings of the plow lay inert on the road and the engine muttered hoarsely to itself.

"You got coffee?" one of the men cried.

"Sure. What have *you* got, John?"

The two men laughed together and kept walking toward the mailbox.

"We have discovered a curve in the road," John said. "You are standing right on it."

"So, have some cake and a meatloaf sandwich, John," Millie said.

"That would be real nice," John said.

"And you, Carl?" Carl Alquist was younger. His blond-red eyebrows were thick as fur above his blue eyes.

"Oh, my wife wouldn't fix me any breakfast this morning. Next thing will be another sex strike, I suppose. You're a couple of heroes around here," Carl said.

Hans smiled and then turned and walked up to the cabin to get rid of the rifle before returning to the group. As he emerged from the cabin he looked off to the left toward the tall cedars where the owl usually perched.

It was gone—for a little while at least.

Love the Wild Swan

Her mother had Lee Blackstad by the wrist as they stood out by the clothesline in the front yard of the house trailer. And her mother wasn't letting go. It was a grip she had used when she tried to make Lee "fess up" and tell the truth when Lee was a little girl. Her mother's face was wide and fat and very close. Her stout body pushed against Lee and made her feel helpless. And the eyes—dark and shiny as a starling's—pressed against Lee's own like two fierce buttons.

"I don't understand you," her mother said, tightening her grip a little more.

"Please, Mother, I don't want to talk about it now."

"No, let me say it. He got you with child and you thought you had to marry him, but you've lost it so why in God's name do you stay here? What is it he has anyway? All of this?" Without letting go of her daughter, Lee's mother swept her free arm around at the little semicircle of run-down farm buildings huddling in weed patches and piles of browning straw beyond the trailer house where the two of them had just had coffee. Somewhere down the little hill that ran toward the lake, cattle bawled and a tractor was droning back and forth out of sight. Her mother looked down toward the sounds. "My God!" she exclaimed. "This isn't rural life; this is exile!"

Lee winced and pulled away, her arm limp, her dress flapping against her thin legs in the wind that swept around the cottonwood trees and kicked up small dust tornadoes on the long driveway running between the farm grove and the edge of a vast cornfield.

"Does the truth hurt that much?"

"It's my tooth," Lee said, lying again, but not quite lying because she had broken off a molar on some popcorn the night before.

"A tooth?"

Lee backed away. For a moment she thought her mother was going to take her jaw in hand and force her mouth open so she could look at Lee's teeth.

"Yes, a tooth," Lee said. "I'm going to the dentist after lunch."

"Oh, Lee!" her mother said. "What is going to happen to you out here?"

While her mother spoke, Lee's eyes were on the clothesline—the pillows. Her mother caught her looking.

"Did you wash those?"

"Yes," Lee said, shifting her position so her back was toward them and her body could shield them from the eyes. God! Pillows. Stained darkly. What a thing she had about clean bedding, her mother.

"I have to fix lunch now," Lee said.

"I suppose you do."

"I do. He works hard."

"Oh, I know," her mother said. "And is it an improvement over lunchroom duty at the school where you used to teach? When you got married you said you couldn't stand things like that anymore and were tired of teaching."

"I had to say something to make myself feel better. I was pregnant. And in the faith of our fathers I could *not* have an abortion, could I? I could just hear little cousin Annie crying, 'My mother said you murdered your baby!'"

"I'm going," her mother said, her eyes glancing past Lee toward the tractor noise, which was getting louder. "I don't want to hear any more of this."

Her mother bussed Lee's cheek with a cool petal of mouth and a fuzzed touch of powdered cheek. Then, her head down and her shoulders hunched, she walked to her car, got in and drove away, her eyes set in a kind of tunnel vision through the windshield, a belt from the seat or her coat or something whipping from under the driver's side door as the car roared away.

It was uncanny—how the tractor, for all its rumbling and chortling, was suddenly there behind her, its red cast-iron front weights only a few feet from her back.

She jumped and heard him laugh. As she turned, her eyes blazing, he shut off the engine so her "God damn you!" cracked loudly in the wind. His smiling eyes grew serious and hard. As always, when he was perturbed, he lifted off the greasy seed corn cap with one big hand and pushed back his dark hair with the heel of the other, his eyes feigning amusement, but darkly angry.

She stood there, arms crossed, defying him. The cast-iron weights on the front of the big tractor were as big as washtubs; they balanced the big plow tilted up behind the tractor.

"You like to scare people?" she cried, walking closer to the weights.

"Lunch ready?" His seed corn cap sat firmly on his head. His dark face was pinched, almost chinless. He had a nervous habit of constantly scrunching his head forward on his neck like a duck or something. "Ugh!" her heart cried. He was a black Norwegian—another one—some gypsy blood or something. He was black, blackened by the sun. He moved his head again at her.

"Lunch ready, honey?" he asked again, forcing a thin grin.

"I'm getting it. It'll be ready in twenty minutes or so."

"I'm plowing up the garden long's I got the tractor here."

"No...." But he had started the tractor and was on his way. He loved to do it. He loved to. She hated herself for it, but she ran after the tractor and the plow. She was a little rag in the procession, her dress—a nice blue summer cotton under the sweater—flapping in the wind. Silly little birdie.

She saw—beyond the chicken house—that he had piled up everything left in the fall garden to form a huge cornucopia in one corner under some leaning hollyhocks—fire-orange giant squash and pumpkins, dark green cones of little ones—acorns—the last harvest before the winter.

She stood, her arms folded, watching it. There was no stopping him. She stood watching the power of it—the steel-shining colters and shares turning the earth so deeply it ached her, turning it into black-blue shining furrows thick and vermicular. The plow ripped the earth, the tractor squatting down on its huge tires with the weights on it, grunting, its exhaust puffing black, then gray, smoke.

"You're packing the earth down deep!" she cried at him and to herself. "That's not good!" she cried. "It goes too deep. It packs too much."

He couldn't hear her, sitting there on the tractor seat, his eyes aiming the power, God damn him. She thought she might lie down in front of it, but it would not just bury her; it would crush her. Some squash vines, only, trailed on the plowshares, then slipped off into darkness. He buried the earth, packed it, left his power on it.

She turned and went toward the trailer house to make his lunch.

She took the pillows with her, ripping them off the clothesline and letting the clothespins snap off or break. She sniffed at one—in a denim striped ticking—his. God how it stunk from the sweat of his head, the stink of his head. She wished she could hide them forever or get new ones. Or burn them—yes!

Inside, on the table she saw all the things her mother had left—cologne, perfume, soap—and the check for $500 for "treats." It was her mother's way—to run to all the children and spread her munificence, to run about oblivious of cause-effect, of past, of things never done to protect them all then—then...the secret. The truth. The father. In his hands....

She slammed the door and fried his lunch. Grease. Oh, and she knew what lunch would be like. She would talk to the top of his head while he ate, while she sat watching him eat and hating the way he did, bread pushing things into his spoon and fork, he savoring the rich gravy.

The phone rang. She ripped it from its cradle. She said to herself, "I ripped it from its cradle" and laughed.

"Hello." It was her mother. "Is *he* there?" her mother asked.

"No."

"You put that check away for yourself," her mother said. "I want you to have it just for yourself. You keep it as your own little secret."

"Yes, Mother. I've got things on the stove."

"I love you, sweetheart."

"Yes, Mother," she said, hanging up, then gagging a little on guilt for not thanking her mother—for not thanking her mother because she did not feel thankful. Too little, too late. Sometimes it is forever too late.

She served Delbert, her husband, seconds after he came in, hung his cap on a doorknob, washed his hands just where she would do dishes and sat down. She could not remember what she said. She remembered only what he said between and through mouthfuls "I see your mother fled the place.... The squash should be cut up and frozen.... You find out what that dentist is going to charge.... And you get me six tubes of grease at the Co-Op! Sometimes I think all those books you read took you away from reality."

"How many?" she managed to ask.

"Six. Say why are you always so goddam angry after she leaves? Why don't you tell her to stay away. No, that's not it either. Why don't you get angry at her instead of me? I could be hurt the way she snubs me, but I got her number. Haven't you?"

He came up to put his arm around her waist as she stood at the sink. She stiffened. He squeezed her, pressed her so hard her ribs ached.

"Your mother just spreads good feelin' and love all over this world, don't she?"

"Please," she said.

"She leave money?"

"A hundred dollars," she said, her chest tightening on the lie.

"Well, I guess I can stand it for a while for that, but tonight we got to get serious. Isn't it near time to try again? We aren't givin' up are we?" He grasped her buttocks with both hands. She tore away and went into the little paneled toilet. Standing there, looking out the window at the starlings waddling in the new-plowed garden and pecking at worms and things she thought, again, about doing it, about letting her blood flow out into the earth. Go back. Go back.

A door slammed, breaking her reverie.

She washed herself. Lifting her arms high to wash under them, she saw her freckles. Always she had seen her own freckles after what her father did. Always she—no—at first she thought it was her own flesh corrupting and spoiling. Spoilage spots. She was not born with freckles was she? Oh, she couldn't remember. But she began to *see* them then. And they were her own fault. They came from within her own self—her own girl-devil self....

She finished washing quickly and put on a gray wool skirt and white blouse and a blue Shetland sweater—the outfit she wore teaching—lit, mythology—all those remote and unreal things. Sometimes her own voice then as a teacher echoed to her now as if she, then, had been smarter and as if she, now, was ignorant—so ignorant she could learn from her former self.

Under the dresser (tipping it up) she found the birth control pills in the packet. She began to take one; then put it back. Her secret; her power. She touched her own stomach. It was flattening and tightening up after the miscarriage. She laughed inside herself. He was a little afraid of her when she was pregnant, why even a little reverent. He loved seed catalogs. He loved his own seed. He was horrified to find out his seed had been dumped—down a sewer by doctors. No wonder he only took her to the hospital and picked her up. Nothing between.

Outside, before she took the pickup, she walked down to look at the lake. It was really a somewhat ugly lake. It was aging, dying. Eutrophication they called it—from all the fertilizer in all the farm fields around it. No swimming there—no clean swimming. Green algae. Green as the fields it was—except in winter. No Walden, no purity.

There were many waterfowl on it—ducks and those things—the coots, the mudhens. Dirty. Sleek. Oil-pelted. Pointed bills. Croaking noises. They dived down into the mud slime. They were hideous. The mallards tilted delicately, their webbed orange feet walking upside-down to keep their heads down—their velvet green heads.

The sun had become hidden by a cloud. The clouds were low and full of wind, feathered like the plumage of some great clean bird.

She knew she would hear it—under, no over, the wind. The grand, joyful silver yelping of the swans—the trumpeter swans. They were there—out far, resting on a band of water grayed by scudding clouds. Their long necks were fine and carved in delicate melodious power. They had come from the north again, from cold Hudson Bay and such places.

"Oh, God!" she cried. "Oh, God, oh my God!"

Guns thumped and ca-rumped on the south side of the lake. Oh, they would not, those men....

She drove much too fast into Odin where Dr. Liv had his office in the old bank building, the Greek revival one, the one with the grand portico, the white architrave, the metopes with fading gold figures.

"Good afternoon, Lee Blackstad," Dr. Liv said, as she stood, finally, deep in the interior of the building after staring up at the chipped pilasters on the front of it and then stumbling on the steps and then following the signs through the vast, dimly-lighted interior to the office where he stood waiting in the doorway.

"Hello," she said, startled by the high-pitched clarity of her voice.

He laughed. "Voices carry in here," he said. "It's the temple of it. Goes up to heaven—it and voices from the Lutheran church of course."

She laughed and tried not to stare at his huge nose.

"I have no receptionist," he said, "so you can come right in. I don't like the idea of a receptionist."

He loomed over her as she stepped past him into the office.

It was marvelous, the office was—all newly done in a light blue, the chair and fountain (gurgling merrily) and cabinets. It was all a vast blue.

She hesitated, but his eyes were kind—then gently questioning.

"I'll need to take a look first," he said. "Would you like to take a seat. I'm a painless fellow except when patients don't tell me the Novocain is wearing off.''

She sat down, felt the white napkin placed softly at her throat, felt the elastic band around the back of her neck (the hair on his hand chilling her down to her toes.) She wanted to get up and run.

The light came down on her face. It revealed all, didn't it?

"I'm freckled," she said.

He laughed. "I am too. I used to think they were blemishes, but my father told me that they are joy spots to break up the monotony of nothing but skin everywhere—acres of it on people."

"Well, I don't know about that."

He worked quickly, his big hands amazingly deft and gentle.

"I'll just about have to cap it," he said. "I can use gold back there because it won't show when you smile—and freckled people have to smile."

"Is it expensive?"

"About a hundred ninety dollars," he said. "That's fair and you must do this for yourself or you'll lose the tooth. You can pay any way you want."

"I'd like that," she said, letting her knees relax a little.

"I have to drill the tooth down and then work down into the gums. I should give you gas or Novocain. Which do you prefer?"

"I don't like gas," she said. "I don't like to go to sleep like that."

"Good," he said. "I don't use it unless someone forces me to."

"How long will it take?" She was tired, sinking.

"Not long and you're my last patient so I can get the temporary cap on today."

While he waited for the Novocain to take effect, Dr. Liv put on a fresh white frock, a starched stiff thing, lifting his arms high as he pulled it down over his head. Then he bent over her and began to work.

A pause. A light. A silence. A rustle of plumage thick and soft. She turned. A raising of giant white wings, plumed wide as the very sky. Breath of flight at the back of her neck. Walls burning. Sails—white—on sea reaches. Air, wind. Engendering with shuddering fall. Clouds, oviform and tumbling down the sky. Watery and soft, the clean of it.

"What is wrong with you?" Dr. Liv was saying then. "My goodness, you are the first patient I've ever had over five who's—whatever. I, I should've asked you if you have seizures or something. You were jumping all over...."

He held the drill away. His eyes were steady and serious and worried.

"I'm all right. Please!" she pleaded. "I'm just a little tired and nervous. I've never had any trouble like this before."

He began to work again. There was some pain. It kept her near to herself. Then, quickly, the clock above them ticking louder, he was done. The temporary cap was on.

"You should have a good physical exam sometime soon," Dr. Liv said, lifting the little white bib off her neck, his hand grazing her cheek (but no chill running through her).

She didn't get up from the chair right away. Above her she could see Liv's ruddy face and the projection of his long nose. When he bent over to look at her, his blue eyes were kind and also shadowed with worry, like a mother's.

He took a clean napkin and wiped around her mouth. "There's a little water there," he said. "You do look a little pale," he said. "I hope you're not worried about all this. It's all going nicely."

"No," she said. "I lost a baby a while ago."

"Ah," he said. "I have no idea what that can be like. What can a man lose that is like that?" He paused. "But, then, do you have some friends— some women friends—to talk to?"

"Not yet," she said. "I mean I don't have women friends like that now."

"I have another young patient—Mrs. Aronson—who lost a child. You...you see we freckled people know what life is really about, but we have to take good care of ourselves—now—not somewhere over the rainbow."

"I will," she said, rising from the chair and letting him help her up.

She made an appointment for a Monday two weeks later, when, by his solemn promise, the gold cap would be ready. When she went out the front of the building she turned to see Dr. Liv standing there between two Doric columns. He looked utterly preposterous—a little like Charles de Gaulle or somebody posing in Athens. She laughed. He laughed and waved goodbye.

As she drove homeward through infinities of corn rows and fences leaning away from the northwest wind, she saw the snow begin to fleece down and mottle the windshield of the pickup, and she wanted to cry at all the emptiness, the hollowness inside her. She pressed her hand on her stomach and let the tears go. But before she drove into the farmyard she stopped and opened the window and let the breeze cool her face.

Shots on the lake. Low, quick thunder ca-rumping.

When she sat in the farmyard and turned off the motor, she cried "Oh! Oh!" to herself, jumped out of the pickup and ran toward the trailer house to get the denim jacket she wore for working outside. She pulled the door open, tugged the jacket off the hook in the lean-to, and, grabbing some canvas which trailed after her in the snow, ran for the garden and the pile of pumpkins and squash.

Strange. A long-handled shovel standing straight up, its blade in the new plowing. And a hole—a little grave—gaping next to it. The green-black plowing was submerging slowly under the whiteness but the black heads of the furrows were still distinct above the calm whiteness.

And she saw him coming toward her out of the snowing, his head down, his neck bobbing a little as it always did when he hurried, his face vague, obscure.

Oh! Dangling from his right hand. Oh! Long neck stretching with each step. The wings folded and soiled, a bloody circle at the breast, the webb-ed feet dragging pitifully.

When he stood by the hole he saw her.

"It's a snow goose," he said. "Probably been dead a long time."

"You're lying!" she said, stepping toward him and taking the wing of it and thrusting her hand into the breast and feeling the warmth, the dying warmth.

She was yelling then. "I'm sick of all the lies," she said. "You shot it, didn't you?"

"No," he cried, his eyes bulging with anger under the cap. "I did *not* shoot it. It fell wounded into the field down there. It was suffering. Now I have to get rid of it. Do you know what the fine is for shooting one of these?—three hundred dollars, three hundred dollars. They don't care who shot it. You got it; you shot it."

"I don't believe you," she said. "Where is the tractor?"

"What?"

She walked past him, her shoes going deeply into the plowing. There, on the tractor in a kind of wooden cradle, was the shotgun.

"You've got a gun," she said.

"God damn it! I didn't use it."

She walked back to the hole. The swan lay in it, curled, crumpled. Its eye regarded her with beady silence.

She pulled the shovel out of the ground and began to fill the hole, madly at first, then slowly and deliberately.

He talked at her. "I can't help it you don't believe no man," he said to her back as she worked. "And you're not the only one who had to live with a father who is god. My father kicked the shit out of me for letting it snow on his squash...."

"Shut up!" she screamed.

"No, I won't!" he yelled.

She swung the shovel up in the air like an ax and let it splat down on the dirt she had piled in the hole.

"Did you get the grease?"

"What? What?" She felt dizzy. Grease? What grease?

She stumbled toward the orange mound of pumpkins and squash, dragging the canvas with her. Then she tried to lay it over them, lifting the edges of the canvas as if she were making a bed.

He took one end and swung it over and put some pumpkins on it to hold it down in the wind. "That'll hold!" he yelled at her. But she wasn't satisfied. She pushed him aside and tried to make the edges even. "You want it perfect in a goddam blizzard?" he cried.

She stumbled toward the trailer and through the little wooden lean-to where they hung their coats. She could hear him following so she hurried. She locked the door from the inside and picked up a long butcher knife and leaned back against the door, glowering at her own muddy tracks on the kitchen floor.

He tried the door. Knocked. Called her name. Hammered. Battered. It held.

"You can't lock me out of my own goddam house!" he cried, leaning against the door on the outside.

Her head was next to one of his seed corn caps. She pulled away. God damn his seed, his planting.

She did it all very quickly. She tilted the painted wooden dresser back and took the birth control pills out and took one with (ish) alkali water from the well. She bathed (the bathroom door locked too) roughly and let the towels fall on the floor. She pushed everything she wanted into suitcases and plastic bags, sliding everything toward the door.

She put on jeans and a sweatshirt (ugh! sweating again) and her high boots. Her mother's check. It was in her billfold.

She stood at the door and listened. Dear God! The howl of his tractor came to her through undulations of the wind. For a second she felt the old—whatever it was.

"No," she cried to herself. "No, no, no!"

She scrawled a note:

66

> *I'll send the pickup back*
> *I'm not at Mother's*
> *Can't come back*
> *Lee*

She backed the pickup against the lean-to. It had a camper on it—a nice cover for her things. She hurried, listening for the tractor between each heave of a plastic bag or suitcase up into the pickup. But the tractor droned and howled steadily, turning the earth, preparing for the seed in the spring.

She looked out from the kitchen window at the front lawn—the one she had tried so hard to grow. The pickup had already left deep, ugly ruts in the wet earth. There would be more ruts after she drove away, but the snow would fill them in and cover them up.

Outside, before she got into the pickup and drove away, she stood in the snow, letting it sting her face. She couldn't see the lake through the veils of the snow falling. She didn't want to. She didn't need to. Surely the swans were gone too.

Whatever: or, I Took My Feminist Friend to the VFW Feed.

I suppose I took Emmie Lee (Lee was her *last* name) to the VFW in my hometown because I wanted to show her off to my old high school buddies. Of course, I didn't tell *her* that. She would've put her hands on her hips and said, "So you think we're dolls you win someplace and show off as prizes, do you?" There were other perils too. The VFW feed has some of the qualities of a mess hall run by ex-soldiers who never quite got enough to eat during their army days. Forget rations, casserole dishes and compotes. Think gargantuan heaps—think *mess* hall—tubs, buckets. Think skillets the size of car wheels and steak knives with the heft of bayonets.

Oh, and then there was Ernie Kowalski—old Yearn Ern as we used to call him when we cruised up and down Main Street in his '47 Merc and he made various primal sounds when girls appeared on the sidewalk. Going to the VFW or anyplace else in Odin meant that sooner or later I would have to—*we* would have to—deal with Ernie—VFW post commander, school board chairperson (that's *my* person) or self-appointed spokesperson for just about anything you could have an opinion on. I could just hear him: "So *this* is your old lady, is it?" or, "This is some petite broad you've brung us!" Then Ernie would find out from Emmie what it was really like to be in a war.

But it was delicious checking into the Bird Cage Motel with Emmie that afternoon—the realization of all my pubescent dreams. She was carrying her own suitcase as usual and the wind off the lake was blowing her skirt very nicely. Very nicely. She walked up to the check-in desk and whanged the service bell with that marvelous assertive energy she always has. Then, after about five minutes, she turned around, smiled. "They all take off for the VFW at the same time?" she asked.

"Read the sign," I said. "It's the same one that was here when Ernie and I painted this place."

Just then she saw the whole entry was full of books lying about on old coffee tables. The manager is always buying books at auctions.

"Is this the county library or something?"

"No," I said. "Jack Nelson was a philosophy prof at Bemidji before he told the president he was a tenured incompetent who could be fired only if he performed unspeakable acts with a badger in a public place."

"Camus," she said, hefting a thick green volume and starting to thumb through it.

"I don't want to be pushy," I said, "but you'd better read the note."

"This is only early Camus," she said, dumping the book into a dusty mohair sofa and then coughing with the dust.

Finally she was reading the note and laughing:

> If you want me I'm in Swanson's Cafe right over
> there across #61 through the big window over the
> mohair sofa. I'll get back in less than 2
> minutes if something doesn't run over me.
> Meanwhile, do some browsing. Some books are to
> be digested, etc.

"That's his ontology," I said.

"I like him," she said. "I haven't met him, but I like him."

I wanted her to hurry. It seemed like she was always getting distracted by things. Me, I was pubescing wonderful scenes in Number 19 which overlooks the park where I also did a lot of pubescing earlier. Ernie and I painted the motel for $400 in 1950 because we thought we'd *see* something through a careless curtain. Ernie only saw an old man apply Preparation H as he bent over in a very undignified way.

She was finally making the call, her voice bright and silver melodic. I could see old Jack gulping the last dregs of Nina Swanson's coffee and rushing off into the path of a semi after hearing that voice.

We waited. I kissed her and held her away from the books. Jack showed up in just one minute and forty seconds, puffing away and announcing the time of his passage. He was tall and yet amorphous in clothes too rumpled and familiar with his body. His face was gray and his cheeks hung down like melting wax. He wasn't saying anything—just looking at us—because he probably remembered why I had painted the motel pink for $400.

He slid a registration card toward her.

Emmie grabbed the pen from his hand and started writing her name.

"We trade off," she said as he handed her a key. "Sometimes he's on top and sometimes I am."

Jack's face turned pink and he coughed, but Emmie didn't see it. She was picking up her suitcase before he could get to it. She walked briskly ahead of me. "If you seem to know what you're doing they won't harass you," she always said before she went on trips.

"It's 19—down to your right," Jack called after us.

She turned. "I'd like to discuss Camus' ethic of cooperation sometime," she yelled back at him.

"Oh, shit!" he muttered, but I cleared my throat then and she didn't quite hear it. I was in a hurry—a terrible hurry. I practically humped her into 19 and onto the bed.

And then tanagers and cardinals flew around in the room—oh, ecstatic bird songs and flowing of willows and water and laughter ripe as the sun....

It was when we awakened that we noticed that someone had put a huge milk pail full of apple blossoms on the end table next to the bed. There was a card hanging from the rusty handle of the pail. Emmie's an insatiable reader. She reached over (waking me up) and took it and then stood up to look at the blossoms and I loved her standing there. She was the answer to the sand rose—the ones along the railroad right-of-way where I used to walk on the cinders, my heart aching down infinite shining distances of rails, the wire humming inchoate love songs in the wind, the delicate sand rose nodding only for me, the....

"Who's EK?" she asked, interrupting my reverie.

"Oh, my God!" I cried.

"Oh, really. *She's* in town for alumni weekend?" Smirking.

"It's Ernie Kowalski," I said. "You know. I've talked about him a couple of times. He's a major figure in the pantheon of Main Street hereabouts."

"A bucket—a pail of tree limbs?"

"We're lucky," I said. "It could've been a box of mice."

"I'm not afraid of mice," she said, standing there naked against the sky.

"Actually this was an incredibly romantic and subtle gesture on his part," I said. "The only thing that came close is when he made a huge valentine in the snow on the hill behind Annie Olson's place."

"With what?" she aked, pulling her clothes on—a gesture that always made me a little sad.

"A manure spreader," I said.

She seemed to stop all motion except to writhe under the blouse she was pulling over her head. "A manure—a manure spreader!"

"Listen," I said. "I'm not defending him, but the alfalfa grew up into a blue-green heart just before their nuptials...."

"Pardon the expression but that whole episode is a pile of you-know-what," she said.

"Well, he won her heart with his artistry," I said, noting her fine legs as she pulled on her shoes. Lord, I am a sexist myself, I guess.

"Babies too, I suppose."

"No, she ran off to Wisconsin with somebody else before that. He's remarried now."

"Fell in love with long distances," she said, kissing my ear and snuggling me as I sat on the edge of the bed.

"You wouldn't believe the sexual fantasies I had about this place," I said. "I often had certain dreams...."

"Oh, yes, I would," she said.

"So, it's off to see Sweet Auburn, loveliest village of the north country...."

"What do they do when they're not having alumni celebrations?"

"They have stump-dynamiting contests and on weekends a few of them take Contac and attempt to operate heavy machinery."

"Oh, dear, let's go," she said.

As we passed by the desk and through the library, Jack Nelson was sitting among his books reading. He looked up for a moment and said, "Solidarity, of course."

"But not as the term is used now," she said, and he bloomed like a big pink rose again. She had him reading. He would read all night, poor guy!

Well, how can I describe my hometown? A catalog maybe...a few salient places and things. In a nutshell (another trope for the place): elms aching for each other as they lean across the street; a Presbyterian church with a low-browed Romanesque portico and a sedate Presbyterian silence; a school resembling, in June, an abandoned penal colony; a General

Motors dealership with a white repair garage and lot full of hulking big cars rural people still prefer to drive; hollyhocks yawning over the lawns; old people rocking on porches or bent in solemn, eternal slow motion in their gardens; the ripple of children's voices from the park; and a street with unmemorable buildings shy as farmers seeking loans. And, of course, the VFW—right next to Gale's grocery. The VFW is a cement block fortress with glassblock windows and an eight-by-eight gold and blue star hanging on the front of it.

It was a lovely evening. I remember Armed Forces Radio in Korea—a song they sang called "My Home Town" with words like, "The folks are the cheeriest in my hometown." Ernie and I went into the army and then to Korea together. Then one day they split us up.

"Either of you have a language?" an officer asked. "I got to send somebody up with the Turks," he added.

Ernie just kind of looked vacant in the eyes. I said, "I've had Spanish."

"That's close enough," the officer said. "You'll do."

So off I went. Ernie was made a supply corporal and that was bad. He never quite forgave me for what happened.

We were approaching the VFW. Emmie squeezed my arm. "Were they all in the war?"

"Kind of," I said.

"What about EK?"

"If you served overseas you can belong."

"What if you cooked or something?"

"You can still belong."

"Well, that seems fair enough. That's more than they do for housewives. They cook for years and don't get the G.I. Bill. The years are just lost for them."

"I learned to shoot artillery fire missions in Turkish," I said, "and how to dig telephone wire trenches and officers' latrines."

I began to mumble to myself because I was afraid she was going to start an argument with Ernie about things like that and, God knows, Ernie spent most of his time in Korea asking combat troops at the PX if they wanted kipper snacks *or* Oreo cookies *or* Chiclets for their monthly PX ration and he was touchy about it. After all, a Korean vet is a war vet. If you're in a country where there's a war going...good Lord! There I was—doing it again for Ernie—anticipating the worst.

"Why are you doing that military stuff?" she asked.

"Because I'm nervous."

"About me?"

"Only about Ernie," I lied.

We were walking by the Presbyterian Church and I kissed her and somebody honked and I felt good because it was spring again—just after school is out—and I'm with the prettiest girl in town and birds are on the wing again....

"It's so crazy," she said, taking my arm and nudging my elbow with....

"I know," I said.

"I mean you get rewarded in a big way in most countries for killing or being able to kill, but for mothering you don't get any official reward and the men with power want to keep you in your place and take your sons."

"*Dulce et decorum est pro patria mori*," I said.

"What is this death-love some men have?"

"I used to hug my M-1," I said trying to get off Leslie Fiedler or whatever oblique reference she was making. "It had a nice walnut cheek," I said, "and shuddered in my arms and was a nympho for Chinese boys...."

"Oh, my God! Sometimes I wonder how we manage," she said.

"So do I," I said. "Here we are—both college teachers and it's amazing because I was the kid that the guys at the Mobil station sent after elbow grease and a left-handed monkey wrench. And I went."

"Now I know why you went too," she said, laughing and bumping me nicely while the elms leaned above the street, aching for each other.

"Hold it!" I exclaimed. "We are about to enter the VFW."

She was shaking her head.

"What if I can't *stand* Ernie K—period?"

"Oh, he'll love you," I said. "You look a little like Elma Kronfus, one of his high school et ceteras of whom he is still fond."

"A little like her?"

"Yes, about one-half."

"There you go again," she said. "A man is solid, husky; a woman is fat."

"Not an ounce," I said. "No fat on Elma, but she had hair like yours...."

Somebody was standing in the VFW entryway leaning against one giant gold spoke of the VFW star and puffing away on a cigar and wiggling his big moustache and beaming all over—not just with his wide, shiny face but with his whole body. It was a kind of total body leer that said, "Aha! I know what you're up to."

"Ernie!" she exclaimed.

"Ernie!" I yelled.

"Greetings!" he yelled. "So you've come to see how the other half lives!"

She walked right into his effusive radiance, took his hand, shook it before he could say another word and introduced herself. His cigar dropped and he caught it with his other hand.

But he wasn't off balance very long.

"Yes, sir!" he said. "You two honeymooners come in and regain your strength."

"We're not married," she said.

His cigar tilted down until he chewed it erect.

"Well, whatever!" he said, "but I have to say I never thought the class goody-goody would be so daring."

"Oh, but when he is bad, he is very, very bad," she said. Walking right past him in that white linen summer dress, she heaved the big heavy door open herself.

Ernie shrugged his shoulders, looked at me and we both followed. As he passed me he said "Whatever" again and I knew there was going to be trouble because Ernie said whatever, whenever he didn't quite get something, and it sounded conciliatory, but believe me, it wasn't.

Inside, they whistled at her; and I, the guy who was so bony-skinny in high school I always looked homemade, felt good. If there were any other women around I didn't see them. It was early. The main crowd would come later.

There they were—all these guys with sunburned, jolly, booze-sanguinous faces—handing her plates and silverware and beer in paper cups. Steaks—slabs of meat that looked like sections of sawed off gray bloody trees flew around and landed on our plates. On the big table there were plastic buckets full of macaroni salad and olives—and, down the line, wedges of cherry and apple pie....

Her eyes popped.

"So much meat!" she cried.

"You'd better believe it," Ernie said, his cigar straight out and one bloodshot eye winking at us.

I was saying "Hi" and "Hello" and "How's she going?" and "Great!" and "Emmie" a dozen times each as we moved towards a distant table to eat. And the guys were nice. Some of them rushed ahead of us and wiped off the oilcloth tabletop and pulled the chairs out and bowed with a phony cavalier formality.

"It is so good to see men doing these things," she said.

Dewey Day was standing behind a chair waiting for her to sit down. She didn't. She said, "I mean it's so good to see men cook and wash things. But I can seat myself. Thanks." Which left Dewey standing there with an incredible nervous gopher grin on his puzzled face. I nodded to him and sat in the chair myself and he fled our table.

But not Ernie. He came over and sat right down and started talking. He had put out the cigar and leaned toward us while we ate—leaned mostly toward her the way he always did when I was with a girl he liked.

"This guy," he began, nodding toward me, "he set records in high school."

"Oh?" She had found something in her macaroni salad. An eggshell.

"Yeh," he said. "He took Bonnie Getz the homecoming queen home after a dance. She lives ten miles out. We timed him. He was back in thirty-two minutes." He leaned back in his chair and guffawed.

She wasn't laughing or even smiling, so he tried to be conciliatory. "Of course, she was a good girl," he said.

"I don't like the idea there are just good girls and bad girls," she said.

"Whatever," said Ernie, fumbling for another match.

A silence—at our table at least. Ernie looked at me the way he looked at me when he found out I was taking piano lessons—oh, and when I decided against going out for football. He was puzzled and maybe angry. If he got up and walked away that meant he was just accepting it—whatever it was—and letting go. I didn't really want that either.

He fired up his cigar again and stayed. By that time I knew then that I was going to be an unwilling witness to combat or resolution or something. She wasn't going to accept him on his terms, that was for sure. And I had regrets because I once told her that Ernie had once carried around—as a daring memento of his first sexual experience—a pubic hair under a plastic card in his billfold.

"It's Victorian," she continued—"those are categories men define. Good girl (she was using two fingers to make quotes on that one) for marriage; bad girl for—whatever. In Victorian London sixty percent of the women were forced into being 'bad' women because they couldn't get either jobs or husbands."

"Jesus," Ernie said. "This is 1980. We're not a bunch of chauvinists. My wife is taking home ec at Duluth. Stays overnight there sometimes and I don't say anything. Could be fooling around with some prof but I don't run over and check it out—except, you know, when I need to go over there for auto parts."

"That's great," I said.

"Does she have a name?" Emmie asked.

"Who?"

"Your wife?"

"Ernestina," he said.

"She was bright," I said.

"Was?" Emmie asked. She wasn't eating much and the guys came over and waved steaks at us and hefted tubs of macaroni salad around and whopped wads of it on my plate where the things congregated like rubbery snails.

"Look," said Ernie. "I'm for equality. I've got no quarrel with you feminists. I told my—my Ernestina that she could go to school and if it didn't get her a job around here she could just keep going to school and maybe do catering or just learn to enjoy super cuisine."

Emmie waved away more macaroni salad and leaned toward Ernie. "But you wouldn't follow her if she found a job in Minneapolis?"

He puffed away extravagantly. "I couldn't," he said finally. "How could I? It's impossible."

"Why?"

He was looking at me and I knew another put down was coming. "I don't know!" he muttered.

"But her education is useless then?"

"Whoa!" I cried, accepting a dozen black olives, more steak and ....

"Keep up your strength," Ernie said, patting my arm. "You'll need it."

It was coming—the put down. "Say," he said, nodding toward me. "You know what his part of the class will read? It said, 'John So-and-So wills his master debating ability to Lawrence Tierney.'" He guffawed again and winked at me—I guess. "It slipped right by old lady Johnson the yearbook advisor," he added.

"That's nice," she said, nestling against my arm. "It relieves a lot of pressure. Women do it too, you know."

He blushed like a big beet with a cigar stuck into it.

"Didn't you?" she asked.

"Well, well...." He puffed madly at his cigar and looked at both the front and back doors of the place.

"You're not a man-hater, are you?" he asked finally. "Some of them are," he added, his cheeks drooping. Battle fatigue maybe.

"Of course not," she said.

"But you don't like small town chauvinists like me, right?"

"You're not," she said. "You're taking time to talk to me and that's nice. All I want is for us all to talk to one another and not use power to exploit each other."

"I suppose," he said. "I suppose."

"When you were in high school could you really talk to girls?"

"We didn't talk to them..." he began, nearly adding, we *did* it to them, but he added, instead, "...we didn't know how."

"So you didn't *know* them?"

"Not really."

"What a shame! You could even marry someone like that the way I did."

"I guess so."

"Well," she said, putting her hand on his, "do you see what I mean? It's just being allowed to be what we need to be and then to know each other...."

Music was playing. For a moment I felt just a little pang of jealousy, but I knew better than to show it. I smiled. The music came from the old Wurlitzer jukebox that had been in the VFW since about '49.

"I love to dance," she said.

"Well," he said, "forget your skinny prof and dance with a...."

"A fat man?"

"A woman is husky; a man is fat," he said, standing up and laughing. We were all laughing.

"Listen," I said, "you dance until the steak and I are a little more compatible. I'm paralyzed temporarily."

I have to admit Ernie danced well and, of course, she could make you feel good dancing somehow because she was always so considerate—as she was in other things. I watched them. He was, undoubtedly, telling her about another one of the romantic fiascoes of my high school days, but I felt good. We would forever play competitive games—he and I—but we were wiser about it. We know enough about each other—our absurdities—so it all cancelled out in a kind of knowing compassion.

She was a marvelous dancer—quick, smooth, right on the beat. She was having a helluva good time. The war was over—for a while at least.

Still, he was probably saying something like, "We gave him an award at our twentieth class reunion—the most improved in looks...."

Whatever.

Cycles

It made both Mona and him nervous because they always wanted goodbye to be a kind of ritual commitment—sweet and maybe a little dramatic. He was a poet of sorts and they were both English teachers. That should mean something. As he stood there looking down at Mona in her blue swimsuit, he could still feel vague, dark pulsings of her body in his and that made him a bit sad. He was about to say, "You're always lovely in your bones..." when the yellow motorbike screamed past them again and leaped around the side of Mona's blue townhouse. Hunter watched it buzz away and fought back a scowl. He had goofed with one son—that one sixteen—in his last serious relationship with a woman— and he wanted to be careful this time.

And there this one (why couldn't he say the name?) came again like an arc of furious yellow light in the morning sun—back and forth, back and forth—creasing the grass, scaring the birds, diverting Mona's attention again and again—especially when he swung his body backward and the front wheel, spinning madly, hovered in the air like a crazed hummingbird....

"Dear God!" she cried. "I do wish his father had waited a couple of years before he bought him one of those."

"Oh, well...." Hunter began. The boy wore a tight smart-ass grin— almost a fornicatory one—a rocking-horse-humping one. Probably living out hero fantasies inside that head.

Hunter almost choked on the patent insincerity of his next words. "Oh, well," he said, "it's tech joy—American boy on cycle."

"I'm sorry," she said, turning over on her stomach just as he sat on the edge of her chaise lounge intending to kiss her and touch her someplace. She was a cosmetic dream—clear, creamy skin. In the morning sun her hair was vibrantly gold—a torch that always started something inside him. Her legs were long and when she turned over she curved her seat upward in a cutely insolent way....

He felt stiff and alien sitting there in summer tans with a briefcase and a travel case between his legs. He felt perched there like a silly bird. Get going! he told himself.

"You're making it hard to go," he said.

"Oh, that's nice," she said. "I never want it to be easy."

She sat up to kiss him goodbye and he felt a surge of anger, he wasn't sure why. Somehow it felt like a small victory for the boy. He held himself back a little from her and saw her eyes go dark and serious.

"Don't you want to kiss me?" she asked.

"Always," he said.

The motorbike zipped by again—a yellow thing snarling.

"I don't think he likes me quite," he said, taking her hand and kissing her forehead. It was salty—sweat. She wasn't supposed to sunbathe with her fair skin.

She held his hand tightly, her eyes still serious. "It's hard for him to see you in his father's place."

"Bed and board!" he quipped. It was a joke of theirs.

"Never bored," she punned. "And bed is lovely."

"It's hard for me, too. I'm used to young people paying attention to me."

"He doesn't know what a professor is—except from the movies, maybe. He doesn't know what you do or anything. Me, he understands—I'm a junior high teacher. But a full professor and tenured...."

"Oh, I'm full all right," he said, feeling better and then a bit foolish for responding even to the flattery.

"We'll probably have to get some counseling for all this," she said. "Everything I've read about combining families suggests it—I mean, if we...."

"No if's," he said. "I've told you...."

"But you look at him like he distresses you."

"I'll work on it," he said.

"We'll have to."

She pulled him to her then and kissed him and he held her for a long time. When he let her go it was quiet—no boy or motorbike in sight.

"There. See."

He touched her shoulder. "Should you take so much sun?" he asked.

"Now don't be a caretaker," she said.

"I want us to be together," he said.

"We will, but just relax a little, will you?"

"I'll try."

"But not too hard."

"When does Gary come from Illinois?"

"At noon." Her eyes were studying his face carefully as she answered him. "Why?"

"I just wondered."

"Well, he pays child support and Tony wants to see him."

"I see. Does he pay?"

"Usually—unless he's laid off for a long time."

"So he just pays sometimes."

"He really does the best he can."

"Well, what can I say?" he said, kissing her fingers.

"It's not great," she said. "He comes on a motorcycle. I make Tony wear a helmet, but I don't like it."

He shook his head. "Maybe I should get one—a big horse of a Harley or something."

"Oh, you're horse enough," she laughed.

"So, farewell, my fancy," he said, leaning down to kiss her.

She smiled and touched his face.

He loved her. He kissed her again.

The boy was watching from the back corner of the garage. Angry. Out-of-gas angry?

So, off to the city with briefcase and night case.

Looking back at Mona, he saw her smiling at him and waving goodbye in a little-girl way, just her hand waving. Lovely torch. Wild nights with thee.

And yet the presence—the boy, the silent machine, his not waving goodbye. The boy was stubby—fourteen—thick dark hair—already a swagger copied from somewhere—a presence of the father. The boy was a small-scale version of his father and that meant that Gary would always be around—and close. What can one do? Mona had had this boy by and with his father. Fact.

"Oh, shit!" Hunter exclaimed as he thought of it all.

Out on the freeway he felt good. The little Toyota was a good car—quiet, reliable—air-conditioned. And he was traveling through familiar country—his home country—pine woods and small farms and quiet towns toward which neat green signs with white lettering pointed. He had taken Mona to his hometown for an alumni reunion—his twentieth. What a beauty! they had exclaimed—and you the guy who had to date Jane Peterson in high school—Jane, Jane—tall as a crane, bony as a cow. A mixed trope—a lousy one for Jane and him.

What the hell! He swung the car off the freeway and up the ramp, stopped, and drove toward Deer Lake—two miles down a tarred road winding through scrub pines and swamp. What for? He wasn't sure, but it made him feel good to think of buying gas at Peterson's Standard—Jane's father's station.

When he edged the car over the hump in the concrete a pickup nearly backed into him; then, jerking on its springs, it drove into the only opening by the pumps. Hunter watched. He felt depressed. The truck driver was a stranger—a big, raw-boned man in western dress—silver buckle, jean jacket, boots. All country western. Dork.

A little blue Chevrolet eased itself away from one of the pump openings and Hunter drove in close to the pumps below the "Full Service" sign.

Hunter was relieved when Mr. Peterson came out, asked "How many?" and began to fill the car.

"Where are you these days?" Peterson asked.

"At UMD."

"Ah!" said Peterson. "So professors all drive foreign cars."

"No," said Hunter, "and before this I tried American cars—tried real hard. I should show you my bills."

"They was going to build a Pontiac plant in Duluth," Peterson said.

"I heard that," Hunter said.

"You got steady work?"

"I'm tenured now," Hunter said.

"Well, we school board people don't like that kind of thing," Peterson said. He wore the same blue coverall and thick rubber-soled shoes and he had the same smile and high forehead, but gray hair now.

"Jane is married to a teacher," Peterson said.

"I heard that."

"She had her troubles too."

Too meant a divorce. Oh, they know a lot about you you don't know they know, Hunter mused.

The pickup truck—its big-bumpered behind high in the air—high as Hunter's windshield—was backing dangerously close to the Toyota. Then it roared away, jumping jerkily through the gears. Why did it back up? That made no sense.

"Hey!" Hunter yelled.

"He's a tough one," Peterson said as the pickup drove off. "He works hard cutting pulpwood by contract. They say don't cross him."

"It seems to me working people are especially angry these days," Hunter said.

"They got reason. When *they* get three months off it's a lay-off."

"I see," said Hunter. "Well, I cut my share of cordwood."

Peterson looked at him—his clothes—his eyes saying, "Huh! You don't look like a working man in that suit."

"What do I owe you?"

"Ten fifty."

Hunter paid cash. Two men stood inside by the pop machine. They looked hot. And their eyes avoided him.

"I don't know a lot of people here anymore," Hunter said.

"You should know them. They built your father's barn."

Hunter shook his head.

"Half the men around here are lookin' for work these days," Peterson said.

"I know that," Hunter said. "That was a main agenda item at our caucus." He took a deep breath. "I may be a college teacher, but I haven't forgotten hard work," he said. "Our Democratic caucus was mostly about unemployment."

"What did that come to?" Peterson asked.

"I don't think I can deliver all that standing out here," Hunter said. Then Peterson was at another car, sticking the hose into it. Oh, he was a sticker all right.

Back on the freeway Hunter let the music and cool air calm him. He was going a steady sixty, the car working quietly—a little world unto itself—like his condo by the campus. He was doing fine. He was safe. So what? Why the guilt?

And then the roaring—heavy roaring with an undercurrent like growling. He looked in the mirror. Behind him, coming up swiftly, was a squadron of motorcycles. On each sat a man with thick, heavy arms that hung loosely on the high handlebars. On the arms, purple and red tattoos. Headbands on big heads—some bandana style. All the faces were masklike, the eyes hidden behind dark glasses. The machines were big ones—their cylinders jutting out on both sides under the legs of the drivers, their cooling fins becoming clearer and clearer as they rode up toward Hunter's car.

He did not want to break the speed limit by too much.

He felt he would like to have a camaraderie with the riders—he who had admired Brando. He slouched a little to appear relaxed, an easy rider himself.

They came on.

Surrounding him, they made a deafening noise.

Close, the chrome handlebars riding close to fenders, windows, mirrors on the car.

A new noise—a terrible one—metal on metal.

They enclosed him in noise and power.

One—a rider with long dark hair tied in a pigtail— was riding on Hunter's left—at the window—on a big machine with jutting spill guards. He reached over, slapped the car, smiled at the squeak of his steel on Hunter's steel.

Hunter held steady, bleeps of fear beating in his head and chest.

And then he hated—hated them for the humiliation, the awful entrapment at sixty miles an hour, the insolence, the brute force—the wolflike rapacity—mindless and cruel and without humor or compassion. They were many and each was big.

They swung two machines in front of him. Their taillights flashing, they forced him to slow down, to pull deeper into the pack. There was nothing on their faces—no smiles, no nothing—deadpan masks.

And he hated.

And then they moved on, howling by him—gleefully it seemed.

He was alone for a few minutes. Then other cars were moving up.

He thought about buying a shotgun in the next town—or calling the Highway Patrol. He could put the shotgun on VISA. Get some shells too.

No.

If he called the Highway Patrol, how could he prove anything? If he did get them into court, who would be his witnesses?

Who cared?

They had had him.

Who could he talk to about all of it?

If he took them to court...who were they? Where had they come from?

He began to shake. They were far ahead of him up the freeway.

He pulled off at a rest stop.

There were about ten cars and vans there from all over the country—families—old couples watering and relieving themselves and their dogs. All of them seemed preoccupied—except one—a young man wearing a Yale U. sweatshirt. He was checking under the hood of a little German car. When he bent over to look at a fan belt or something the shirt separated from his O.D. pants to reveal a very hairy torso.

Hunter tried to talk to him.

"Did you see the bikers?" he said.

No answer.

"They surrounded me out there and one of them forced his machine against my Toyota. It was pretty scary. Scratched one fender pretty badly."

The young man bumped his head as he raised it. "Shit!" he exclaimed. He slammed the hood down, got in the car, backed it past Hunter and drove off.

For a while Hunter sat in his own car and watched the travelers for no particular reason. The gouge on his left front fender was like a cut into him—a fresh, painful one still bleeding.

When Hunter drove into the garage beneath his condo he shut off the car and sat there quietly. He felt exhausted. He had to call somebody.

Upstairs in his bedroom he dialed Mona. No answer. He showered and changed clothes. Then he dialed again. It was 2:30. Where was she? With them? Hardly. Not three on a motorcycle. He let the phone ring a long time. Finally a voice—the boy's—a hoarse, slightly squeaky one.

"Hi, is Mona there?"

"No, she went with Dad."

He forced a laugh. "On his motorcycle?"

"No."

"Just kidding," he said. "Tell her I called."

"Okay."

Funny. The voice sounded lonely.

He had a perverse, a terrible impulse to blurt, "Say, Tony, I might buy a motorcycle," but he said, "Take it easy," instead.

He felt sick. Where was she?

At 3:00 he called his insurance agent. The agent lived in the group of condos next to Hunter's. His agent's name was Bill. Bill's voice was cheery and reassuring on the phone. "Why don't you come up," Bill said. "We're watching bad TV—the wife and I. I need a break."

Hunter took the elevator down and walked over to Bill Thornbeck's condo. As he walked along the wide sidewalk that joined the units, Hunter felt a bit dizzy. Down the hill to his left the traffic moved briskly along the shore of Lake Superior.

Where were they? he wondered. Where did they come from?

Women are assaulted. The thought occurred to him.

He was glad to see an insurance agent for once in his life. Thornbeck's place was exquisitely furnished and arranged.

Thornbeck was very understanding and appreciatively horrified. His wife paused in her stirring of things in stainless steel bowls and looked with compassion at Hunter as Hunter related the details of the occurrence on Interstate 35. Thornbeck shook his head from time to time in believing disbelief. Finally he put his hand on Hunter's shoulder and said, "Those kinds of people do those things—maybe to give meaning to lives that don't mean much, I don't know. At any rate you did the right thing to keep your cool the way you did. We'll get your car fixed up for you, but the distress we can't compensate you for, unfortunately."

Hunter felt relieved and blessed. It was like a blessing. Thornbeck, who was lighting a large brown pipe, wore silver-rimmed glasses and tan safari pants. He was in his sixties. His eyes were blue and candid. All in all, he seemed quite fatherly.

"Thanks," Hunter said. Then he went into the kitchen and said thanks to Mrs. Thornbeck, who had served him two cups of coffee. She shook his hand and touched his arm gently, soothingly.

In the elevator on the way down from the Thornbecks', Hunter wondered if he should even bother to call Mona. She made him angry. She had been married to one of them, he told himself several times. The thought of it. So she went to school. So she changed. Where was she? Well, that was obvious. But what kind of where? His place? It was humiliating all in all. There were plenty of single women in other condos—hell—within walking distance—and college teachers—Alice B. from Princeton. That whole thing down there with the kid and the father. It was a lot to ask.

He wondered if he was the man for Mona—the proper agent.

Then the old depression hit him again.

He dialed again at 8:00.

The boy answered—as gruffly as he could manage.

Hunter hung up without talking.

At 9:00 he fell asleep reading his own report on strategic planning in the humanities department.

When he awoke it was 11:00. He didn't have the energy to call again. He was angry. Damn kid. His mother and father created him. That gave them an eternal bond in the blood.

Still, Mona was lovely.

Where was she?

What if she was with him—her ex?

You're going round and round and round, he told himself. You've got to break out of the circle.

He forced himself up and grabbed the phone and dialed Mona's number again.

Nobody at all answered.

He let it ring again and again and again—the same noise. He put the phone down and dialed again to make sure he had the right number.

No answer.

Was the boy asleep?

Where were they, for God's sake?

He decided that he would not be humiliated like this again—ever. Junior high indeed.

He drank half a glass of Cutty Sark.

He decided he would never call again or go there.

Then he wondered how he could explain why he called early in the morning when he called early in the morning.

It goes on and on and on, he decided.

Maybe there was an explanation for everything—an acceptable one.

Horse. Where did she get that idea?

The Scotch began to make him drift in his mind—a euphoric drift to nowhere in particular. After a while he slept badly.

Indian Sofa

Slim Jim Hayes spun around in his orange swivel chair and glared at Jimmie Dorn. It was a chair he kept on the loading dock exclusively for himself. When he sat in it to talk to Jimmie and Bud or anyone else for that matter he sat in it as the official, not-to-be-argued-with owner of Slim Jim's Economy Furniture Store.

"No, I'm not kidding!" he said to Jimmie. Hayes was a chubby little man with horn-rimmed glasses and a rubber-tough purple mouth. SJ, a lot of people called him. People called him a lot of things.

"But *we* didn't sell it!" Jimmie said. "And I thought the bank carried the paper on installment furniture. So why are we...."

"You thought! You thought!" Hayes' eyes were bulging with anger. He grasped the arms of the swivel chair like he might spring out of it and attack. "That's the trouble with you college kids. Think. Think. Think. This ain't no school. I've got to pay bills and keep a business going. She's missed three payments—three!" He held up three crusty fingers.

"But...." Jimmie tried to sit down somewhere. "But..." he began, trying to park his tired body on a short stack of boxes. He was trying to rally himself.

"Don't sit!" SJ yelled. "Those are lamps—glass—for God's sake! The light of the world!"

"Sacrilegious!" Jimmie muttered, jerking his seat off the boxes.

"Go!" SJ yelled. "Get Buddy Boy and go! This should be a piece of cake for you—a piece of cake. A great assignment for football players—so go *tackle* it!"

"It's a woman!" Jimmie protested. Oh-oh, SJ was getting a depressed look on his face and beginning to growl deep in his throat...whew!

So muttering to himself, as SJ growled, Jimmie stepped into the semi-darkness of the store to look for Bud Olson.

Bud was there by the infant cribs, his big hands working tenderly at assembling one of SJ's new "Night-Night" cribs that sold for $39.95. Bud was all biceps and thighs and muscle. He was swearing at the pink crib because his hands were too big for the tiny screw driver he was using, but he was really a good-natured guy. Jimmie looked at his broad back and was reassured.

"We have to go and retrieve a sofa," Jimmie said. "I need you to run a little interference for me or something."

"Skip the odious athletic analogies, my boy," Bud said, lifting the assembled little crib up into the light and looking through its slats at Jimmie. Whenever Bud didn't want to get too serious he began to talk like W.C. Fields—his voice droll and nasal.

"You see, my dear fellow, we are all prisoners of fate," Bud said through the pink slats.

"SJ is our fate," Jimmie said, "and a red sofa is our destination."

"I believe," said Bud, "that the frightful thing is in the sole possession of a noble woman by the name of Margaret Beargrease who resides in the Indian Nation and had the misfortune of being sold a bill of goods."

"I have the impression that if I don't go and get it I will be unemployed. If you don't go with me, you too, may suffer dire consequences...."

"This whole job is a dire consequence, my boy."

"So," Jimmie continued, "I think we will have to get us into yonder truck and go out and replevin it."

"Now?" Bud had put the crib down and had reverted to his usual soft and gentle voice.

"Now. Hit 'em when they're still groggy from sleep."

"I'm groggy from sleep too," Bud said. "You sure there's no other way?"

"You still here?" A very loud voice crackled over the vast prairies of mattresses surrounding Bud and Jimmie.

"We're going!" Jimmie yelled back.

"No havee sofa at ten, you no makee any more yen!" Slim Jim cried.

"Not bad," Bud, back in his Fields voice, said to Jimmie, "but a certain ethnic slur is there too. Prejudice inheres in language, the vehicle of cultural values...."

"Move your butts!" Slim Jim yelled.

"Hurry up!" Jimmie exclaimed, taking the keys to the furniture truck off the key-board at the back of the store. Bud followed.

"Ten!" SJ yelled after them.

Slim Jim's truck was an old army deuce and a half with rusty ribs arching over the box bed. In wet weather the canvas cover could be pulled over everything but that morning it lay crumpled just behind the cab. The words "SLIM JIM'S ECON. FURN." were blazed in red paint along both sides of the truck bed and on the cab doors. Since the truck was painted white and Slim Jim had done the lettering it all had a certain erratic bloody calligraphy about it. Jimmie drove.

"White!" Bud yelled over the roar of the engine.

"What?"

"White!" Bud yelled. "We are going to violate the territorial integrity of...whose goddam sofa is it? We're going to do it in a *white* truck?"

"A Mrs. Beargrease."

"And Mr. Beargrease?"

"None."

"Sons and various warriors?"

"Unspecified."

"You're not supposed to just drive in," Bud continued. "As I recall from my ethnic American cultures course, you're supposed to stop at the edge of the village; develop a certain dialogue—perhaps with gifts...."

"It's not a village," Jimmie said.

"The element of surprise?"

"Oh, it'll be a surprise, all right."

As the truck roared up Devil's Track Lake Road toward the Chippewa settlement north of town both Jimmie and Bud fell into profound dejection.

"For this I read the greatest minds of all time," Bud muttered. "Now I discover I have had a defective reality principle."

"For this I need your muscle to help me hoist the sofa," Jimmie said.

"They wouldn't...."

"I doubt it. They're really very kind and peaceful."

"She's big? Little?"

"I don't know."

"Armed?"

"I don't know."

"And the color of the beast?"

"It's red—like I said—three-cushioned. It went at $299—discounted.

It's made like $99. He marked it *up*, not down. Really."

"Can we hurry?"

"We're just about there," Jimmie cried, seeing the little rows of brown-gray houses tilt up toward the windshield as he drove down an incline and then urged the old truck up a long hill through the birches and poplars.

"It's a gorgeous day," Bud said.

"Not for St. Sebastian," Jimmie said.

"That's terrible. That is a terrible quip."

There were only a few children playing around the houses.

"I've never been in one of these places," Jimmie said.

"Neither have I."

"They could all be in a meeting," Jimmie said. He was grinding the old truck down into super low, letting it move along muttering to itself in its exhaust.

"Which one is hers?" Bud asked.

"The one with the red sofa," Jimmie said.

"If there's more than one?"

"One what?"

"The Aristotelian categories!" Bud said.

"Old Prof Loken never said that."

"Old Loken never had to enter a Chippewa village and confront a tribe. And us in a white army truck too. An overt hostile action."

"There it is," Jimmie said.

"Where?"

"On the mailbox."

"Right. M. Beargrease. Go check it out," Bud said. He was being hearty and generous.

"I'm the *driver*," Jimmie said, looking down into the smiling brown faces clamoring at the truck cab—hands above the faces waving wild flowers....

"Oh, Lord!" Bud cried. "We come to take while they give."

"Anyway," Jimmie said, "we'll flip a coin to see who goes in. Tails I don't go, heads you do."

"Heads!" Bud said.

Heads it was.

"Oh, I'll go with you," Bud said. "We've been through thick and thin on the old gridiron et cetera."

"Sports analogy."

"I know," said Bud, shoving the door open.

They both stepped down from the truck at the same time and then they closed their doors gingerly, wincing at the clicks of the locks.

The yard was unmowed but neat. A wide riot of Indian paintbrush flowers filled the yard—except under the trees.

"Go ahead and knock," Bud said, leaning over and nearly going into his football guard stance, then straightening himself.

A face appeared at the screen door—a wide, round face with deep lines in it—a face so wise Jimmie had nothing to say to it.

Bud's voice over his shoulder: "We're sorry. We're just college guys trying to—well—old SJ told us we had to get your—that—that sofa."

"Sorry." Jimmie's voice was a hoarse echo of Bud's.

She opened the door to let them in. Jimmie turned a silly, surprised face toward Bud; then motioned him in.

The sofa was right there in the kitchen along one wall. The kitchen was neat and clean. A little gray table sat by the big wood stove and a bouquet of flowers waved gaily from a vase on it. They all stood looking silently at the sofa.

She went over and sat on it and folded her arms. She was wearing a heavy green chamois shirt, brown work pants and trail boots. She looked strong and competent.

"Mrs....?" Jimmie's voice was tremulous and vague.

"Take it," she said quietly.

"But, Mrs...."

"Please stop calling me Missus," she said. "My name is Margaret. I have an identity of my own. And whether you realize it or not, native American culture is matriarchal even though it is not matronymic."

Bud leaned heavily against the little refrigerator by the door.

Jimmie sat on one arm of the sofa.

"I'll be darned!" Bud said finally.

"You see," she said, "I wish to protest thirty-six percent interest and cheap furniture. If you would just pick up me and the sofa and transport us both to Jim's, I would be satisfied. And, after all, you will have retrieved the sofa."

"But won't it be undignified?" Jimmie asked. "I mean...."

"The worst indignities are the silent, invisible ones—the poverty—the abuse of the helpless. You see, I didn't even buy or begin to buy this for myself. It was for a friend who is somewhat blind and cannot quite experience subtle color...." Her eyes observed them calmly as she spoke.

"You want us to bring you back too!" Bud exclaimed.

"What about people here?" Jimmie asked.

"Oh, they'll look away until I'm gone."

"Could you walk to the truck?" Jimmie asked.

"No," she said. "And it would be most gracious of you to hurry."

"Maybe we should call SJ," Jimmie said.

"With what?" Bud's face was strained and anxious and beads of sweat stood out on his forehead.

"I want you to understand that I perceive this as an opportunity to protest. I'm doing this as a consumer too," she said.

"Well," said Bud. "I suppose we'd better give it a try."

It was a terrible wrestle with doors and sofa legs and cushions. They took Margaret and the sofa a few feet at a time. The worst was getting both of them up into the truck. Finally she did climb up and they got the sofa up there too. Then she sat, facing in such a way that in town Lake Superior would be on her back; the fronts of the businesses would be facing her.

"I know why you're sitting that way," Jimmie said.

"Good! Good!" she cried, settling down into the cushions.

They looked at her for a moment. There was a calm about her sitting there in the sofa, her hands folded over one another.

"Are you ready?" Jimmie called to her.

She nodded.

They drove carefully, easing over bumps and starting out from stop signs slowly. They didn't talk at all, but from time to time both looked back to see her sitting there in stony repose on the sofa.

On Main Street they drove faster, but not fast enough. People pointed at them; merchants came out of their stores to squint in the sun and then shake their heads. Children shrieked, "See the Indian lady!"

By the time they got to Slim Jim's, SJ was waiting for them, pacing back and forth on the loading dock—back and forth.

When the truck drove up and before Jimmie could begin to back it in, SJ was tugging at the door on Jimmie's side.

"What the hell is this?" he cried, his face flushed and sweaty.

"The sofa," Jimmie said.

"I didn't tell you to *kidnap* anybody for God's sake!"

A slow and ancient voice spoke then—from above—from the sofa.

"I was not kidnapped, Jim; I came of my own free will to protest your thirty-six percent and the shabby quality of this—this sofa."

"What is this anyway?" SJ asked Jimmie. "My God! I just run a little business. I don't want to take on some kind of rights movement."

"Slim Jim, you are nothing more than a little fat cat," Margaret chanted from above. "Under the guise of benevolent small-town good-old-boy this and that you sell bad furniture."

SJ leaped up on the running board on Bud's side.

"You get her out of there!" he screamed at Bud.

After they backed the truck over to the loading dock, Bud and Jimmie eased Margaret and the sofa off the truck. She sat quietly and looked steadily at SJ. He stood, his hands on his hips, staring back at her, his eyes nearly bulging his glasses off his face.

"The frame is already coming unglued," she said, patting the edge of the sofa with one hand.

"So's he," Bud muttered.

"You get working!" SJ yelled. He began to pace back and forth. "I'll deal with you later."

Jimmie turned to SJ. "What about Margaret?" he asked.

"Who?"

Jimmie nodded toward the sofa. "Margaret Beargrease."

"Oh," SJ muttered, "—oh, now I get it. Well, well, so our little liberal college boys are doing good deeds—consumer protest, is it?"

"That's nonsense, Jim!" Margaret said. "They've been so nice that I couldn't think of legal action or anything. And goodbye. I've made my point."

SJ gasped at her words. "What? What do you mean?" he cried.

Margaret was stepping down from the sofa and then the loading platform. Without another word, she walked down the alley in the direction of her village.

"You can't walk all the way home!" SJ yelled after her.

No answer.

"You see she gets a ride home," he said to Bud and Jimmie. "She could get hit or something."

"She doesn't *want* a ride," Bud said.

SJ was examining the sofa. "Let me see," he said. "I got nine payments. I may do all right if I fix it up a little. Have a reconditioned sale in late August."

"Everybody in town's seen this one," Jimmie said. "You won't even have to advertise."

"Go to hell!" SJ said.

"Now that's an interesting theological imperative," Bud said. "The question is...."

"This ain't no seminary," SJ said. "You two get that damn sofa out of my sight. Take it in the shop. It's all unglued."

"Unglued, unglued," said Bud, his voice a W.C. Fields nasal drone.

But they didn't go into the shop. They both ran down the alley toward the street where Margaret Beargrease had disappeared. As they ran around the wall of the drugstore they nearly ran her over. Then they began to walk in stride with her.

"We'd like to walk you home," Bud said.

"If you wish."

"We'd like to talk to you."

"But not about the sofa," she said.

"No, just maybe about things," Jimmie said.

Above them gulls veered off the sun-danced waters of the big lake and swung over them crying. At the curb ahead of them three or four Indian men sat in a black Chevrolet watching.

The three of them—Bud, Jimmie and she—walked on past the car. Then they heard booing and hissing.

"Look at the nice boys who work for a crook!" one of the men yelled.

"Not any more," Jimmie said.

"Don't try to explain," she said. "Let us simply enjoy this walk together."

Hanson's Bull

During the auctioning I could see Hanson standing there by that old rust-eaten pickup truck I've seen parked in town a thousand times. His arms were crossed one over the other and from time to time he kicked at something on the ground. He was a big man with a round barrel of a chest under his black suit. His neck was thick and his hair—even at sixty or so—was sleek, gunmetal blue-black. He used to fight by butting his head. Two years ago a fighter from Duluth broke both his hands on that head. Me—I'm a frail man—indoor life in the bank I suppose. I never fight.

Once, just as they were going to auction off the last of his cows, he honked the squawky horn of the pickup and scared the hell out of the two cleanup men who were herding the cows up to the fence so people could see them better. The two of them stiffened up and stood there looking a little scared, but I wasn't afraid of him; I was afraid *for* him. His neighbors said he was keeping too much to himself, not even going to town to Augie's Cafe. There had been a couple of suicides by farmers who were losing their farms. They were loners too.

"Louis," I said, walking up to the pickup, "do you think you ought to be watching this?"

He didn't even look at me. He was looking off into the grove at something.

"You see that chipped old porcelain pot layin' off by the hayrake?" he said.

"Where?" I asked. I had to be careful I didn't patronize him.

"I told you where."

"I couldn't see it."

"She used to make good egg coffee in that," he said.

"I've had some," I said, "—a couple of times."

Then he was kind of sniffing at something and I saw what—lilac bushes heavy with violet blossoms leaning against the porch of the farmhouse and nodding in the wind off the big lake.

"And now they are in the dooryard blooming..." he said. I didn't know what to say then with him talking funny like he did sometimes when we were in school together. I just wished we could get it over with sooner.

"Those were tender years," he said, somehow reading my mind.

"Yes," I said.

"Before you took up banking," he added....

"Well," I said, "banking took me up or my father did."

"Sure, and you didn't want to."

"I guess not."

"You wanted to be a musician or a preacher or something."

"I guess so."

"I just wanted to be a farmer. I just wanted to walk out on some land and see how it was doing. I just wanted to worry about it if it wasn't doing well or feel good if it was...."

"Well," I said, walking over and putting one foot up on the running board, "you've had about forty years of doing what you wanted to do at least. That's more than I...."

Damn! Out of the corner of my eye I could see the cleanup men leading Hanson's team of sorrels out of the barn. They were fine horses—sleek and well cared for. Their hooves were quick and their backs rippled tan-brown in the sun....

"Damn it!" I exclaimed. I was frustrated at the timing.

He was watching too as the team trotted out at the end of the long black reins the slim man held. Then they were left standing out in the sun, stomping their hooves at flies and at times twisting their heads back to bite at them.

"Sons-a-bitches coulda sprayed them," Hanson said.

"I'll go down and tell them," I said.

"Oh, Mr. Banker, don't you bother," he said.

It hurt when he said that. He was two classes ahead of me at Odin High. I've sat in church with him and, God knows, knelt next to him when his knees thudded down at the communion railing and that big hand was held palm up for the wafer.

"So I'm Mr. Banker now?"

"Something like that."

"Well," I said, "I tried everything, but the board...."

"Sure," he said, "—the board. It's a funny board, though; you didn't sit on it; it sat on you."

"I'm not passing it off on the board," I said. "I was the loan officer who gave all the credit...."

"...at eighteen percent," he said, "but I know your motives were otherwise pure."

"Not really," I said, trying to keep track of the cleanup crew down there below us at the bay on the lake. They were backing a big cattle truck toward a pen on the other side of the barn.

"It won't work," he said.

"What won't?"

"What they're doin'."

"What do you mean?"

"He won't go. He likes the smell of where he is—all kinds of heifer and cow manure—and the hay too. That's his home and his love-pen...."

"Here," I said, handing him a cup of coffee poured from my thermos. He took it. Sipped. Frowned at it. "Crankcase oil!" he exclaimed. "Who made this piss?"

"I did," I said.

"It tastes like bachelor coffee," he said.

"Well," I said, sipping some myself, "you had about forty years of good coffee. I never did."

"Oh, that wasn't the best part," he said.

Well so he married Naomi Peterson, the first girl I ever loved—or thought I loved. She was willowy and tall and had eyes so wide and bright you forgot she had wonderful high breasts and long legs. But she was dead so neither one of us had her anymore.

"They don't give a damn," he said.

"Who?"

"Any of them—the men you got down there who don't know anything about a bull's territory and the son-of-a-bitch Tilsen Farms businessmen who have about as much feeling for the land as one of those airliners flying over (he nodded upward and sure enough...) from Denver or wherever."

"It's business now," I said.

"Sure," he said, "but it used to be farming. It used to be I could walk behind my team and smell the turn of the earth and step along in a new furrow along with gulls and such and lie down in it if it was warm and my ulcer hurt. Now your boys sit up in a tractor cab and listen to a goddam radio...."

"You were right, you know," I said. "You farmed with an old tractor and some horses—put a lot of labor into things—kept your overhead down...."

"Labor intense," he said, his voice sharp-edged with sarcasm, "and then, with your blessing, I helped my son-in-law buy all that land at a thousand an acre...."

"Sure," I said. "We thought that with a limited amount of land it could only go up."

"Some economist told you."

"Told us," I said.

"Oh, it's my fault too," he said. "My father blamed old Hoover back in the Depression. But this isn't a depression so it's my fault too, I suppose."

"It's international things," I said, "—Brazil, Argentina—Australia. Things change."

"I didn't, so where does that leave me?"

"You could run my farm," I said before I wished I hadn't.

"You can run yours up yours!" he said.

"Where are you going to go?" I asked. I had noticed that there was a hose lying in the back of the pickup with some other things. I didn't like the idea of his sitting here after we left. We'd had problems on another farm. There had been a hose in the back of another pickup. That farmer had hooked it up to the exhaust.

"Nowhere," he said.

Oh, about that time there was a terrible commotion, all right. There was that big Black Angus bull all turned around and hunched up—in the chute running up to the back of the cattle truck. He was mad, the bull was, the whites of his eyes showing and his long tongue stuck out at the two cleanup men as if to say, "No you aren't" while they were poking at him with those electric prods.

You see, it's impossible for a bull to turn around in one of those chutes but he was doing it and then, quick as a bank withdrawal in the Depression, he was galloping back into the pen and picking his hooves up and braying like a mule.

"He don't want to go," Hanson said at my elbow.

"No kidding," I said.

The two cleanup men were sitting down panting and muttering and swearing at the bull who was standing there sniffing at the air.

"He's testy," Hanson said. "He hasn't had any for months because you took my cows and heifers too. Now all he has is sniffing. The pen is full of their smells."

"My God!"

"You could take his balls and even that wouldn't do it. He'd still have memory."

"I don't like the way they use those prods," I said. "I don't suppose I could talk you into helping them. It might save hurting him."

"They hurt him they're going to deal with me."

"I know. That's what I mean."

"Horatio had his day," Hanson said, "and he was appreciated."

I looked at his face then. There was something else there for just a moment or so—his old ironic droll comic sense—the one Naomi loved—along with his other—well...attributes, I guess. Anyway I listened.

"You see," he said, "Miss Goanson was told she had to have her cow Gracie serviced. Well, she put it in a truck and brought it over and well, I didn't watch and she was too bashful. Anyway two weeks later the cow was acting frisky so up into the truck they put it again. And then the same thing happened two weeks later. 'Well,' her sister says, one morning, 'can you see Gracie?' 'Yes.' 'Does she look serviced?' 'No, but she has climbed up in the truck all by herself and is waiting.'"

I laughed and he smiled.

"Some never get enough," he said, looking at me, not smiling. Then I knew I had to get it over with. I walked down to talk to the cleanup men. They were discouraged and angry.

"Can you lead him at all?" I asked, looking into the pen where Horatio stood munching on something.

"Funny thing is," Slim, the tall one, said, "you can lead him around because he's been a show bull but he can tell that truck is going to take him away."

"That's about it," Butch, the stocky blond one, said.

We were standing there trying to figure out what to do when I got an idea.

"Say," I said. "Slim, I've got an idea. You lead him over there under the front overhang on the barn. Feed him something good, et cetera.

Butch, you get that team over there (it was hitched up to pull a wagonload of stuff to town); hook it up to the hay rope; we'll put the hay harness on him and pull him up and back the truck under him. Then we'll lower the rope and we'll have him."

"I'm willin' to try anything," Butch said. "I got my girlfriend to pick up at 3:00. And that's no bull!"

I felt good. I might be a banker, but I had some savvy too about country things.

It all went nicely. Slim led Horatio out, clucking to him like a mother hen and saying, "We're gonna get you some nice oats and a hot heifer." Slim had some manure on a mat of hay and must've hit the smell just right because Horatio was sniffing and whipping his tail around and coming right along.

But even the best laid plans, etc.

They got the hay harness on Horatio and the horses stood about fifty feet away, all hooked up to the hay rope and ready to help Horatio make his ascension. "Git up!" Butch said and the rope tightened on Horatio's belly and his tail stuck out stiff and he humped into the rope....

Just as his hooves came off the ground Horatio let out a bellow like a diesel truck. The horses whinnied, threw their shoulders into their harnesses, the long hoist rope tightened and Horatio went straight up into the air, humping and bellowing. Then the hay sling carrying him hit the rail that runs into the haymow and Horatio disappeared, the pulleys on that sling shrieking so it froze my blood. The whole roof of the barn sagged, and you could see just where he was by the shingles popping and flapping down the roof. Then, when the sling hit the back of the haymow it ripped and there was a terrible thud and bellow when Horatio plummeted into the hay.

"Lord God of Mercy!" Slim cried. "We have sent him to hay heaven!" I could see Hanson had swung open the door of the pickup and was standing there looking like he might charge at all three of us.

"You better not have killed him!" he yelled.

But we could hear Horatio stomping around up there and huffing and bellowing. Butch had calmed the horses down by then and came running over to us where we stood under the hayloft overhang. "I've heard of sending studs out to pasture," he said, "but, by God, this will be somethin' to tell at Augie's tonight."

"Why, he's got everything up there except heifers and water," Slim said. "It's the height of material prosperity."

"Oh-oh," I said, seeing Hanson coming down toward us, his thick arms swinging at his side in that old black suit.

"I don't want no fights," Slim said. "I ain't paid to get killed."

But I could see Hanson had a smirky grin on his face and was thumbing some Viking snuff into one side of his teeth—something he never did before a fight.

"Well, boys," he said, "you have really got him pissed and my team looks like it would like to gallop off to Canada. You have got yourself a real *live stock* problem."

"I'm afraid it was my idea," I said.

"I figured as much," he said.

"I'm not sure what to do next," I said, half-leading.

"Well," he said, "you could take the barn apart if he don't. Then again you may have to shoot him, which is logical since you've taken away everything still alive on the place except rabbits and such. That's about right for your goddam corporate farm. Those goddam corporations got no body or soul. They really ain't alive if you know what I mean. They don't want to bother with people; they just want the farm to be another grain and chicken machine."

He left then. As he walked up to his pickup he cut himself a lilac sprig with his jackknife and held it up to his face like he was kissing it goodbye.

"I feel like shit!" Slim said.

"I got to get to town by 3:00," Butch said, looking at his watch.

We stood there watching Hanson drive away. He wasn't looking back.

"I'm leavin'," Slim said.

"What for?" I asked.

"I'm ridin' with Butch and the team into Odin. We'll barely make it in by 3:00."

"You're supposed to finish the job," I said.

"We did," Butch said. "We did everything you told us to. But some things is beyond the call."

"Well," I said, "I guess I had this coming, but I just don't know how I'll get that bull to town."

"You could put him in the trunk of your Buick," Slim said, grinning at Butch.

"Sure could," Butch said. "A lot of bull has been hauled in that car the last couple of years."

"You could call Doc Liv, the Mayor. He could maybe pull him out," Slim said.

I shrugged my shoulders and let it go. One thing I've learned about people up here: don't start nagging or threatening them. They might be poor and there might not be any other work around, but they won't take it.

"Old Hanson'll be drunk tonight," Slim said, "so maybe I'm going to enjoy a night at home with the wife and the kid. Get ready for church and things."

"He'll be in church with all of us on Sunday," Butch said. "It's his turn to usher."

"The church is for sinners, the pastor said. You comin' too, banker?" Slim asked.

I shrugged my shoulders. They weren't talking just to me anyway. When the two of them drove that team away pulling a grain wagon, it was like something in history was driving away and that made me sad. On the back of that wagon in blue letters was "Hanson Farm."

After they left I was alone on that farm nestled in white pines off the big lake. Hanson had put in the crops and the wind was sweeping through the oats and barley and buzzing through the old buildings. I jumped when a screen door flapped on the front porch of their house. The house looked crippled and old. Its porch sagged and the roof was moss-rotted and black.

I climbed up into the barn loft on a moldy, dusty old ladder. Oh, I was careful. I just peeked slowly over the edge of the hay. I could hardly see into the dark up there. The pigeons had come back and were cooing somewhere above me. A beam of sun, all full of dust, leaned across the darkness. I could gradually see that there was about three feet of hay up there except at the back end where Horatio dropped. There it was about five feet deep.

Except for the doves cooing it was quiet up there and a little scary too. As I looked, I finally made out Horatio in the shadows. His sleek Black Angus coat was matted with dust and straw. He was just standing there a few feet away looking at me.

Jonah

He hurried to dress and to find some cash to take with him to Duluth. He swore because the pastor was coming over and he didn't want him to. My God, what a phone call that was anyway. "You should talk to somebody about things, don't you think?" the pastor kept saying. "What's to talk about?" Jonah kept saying. "She screwed that son-of-a-bitch behind my back and I am divorcing her, that's all. And her bawling and all her damn relatives won't make me change my mind."

Then the pastor said, "I'm not coming over to try to get you to change your mind. I'm coming over to give you some company. And maybe have a cup of coffee with you."

"Well, I ain't making coffee so you better try the Scandia." But no use.

"I'm coming over," the pastor said—hounding him like a damn life insurance salesman. And, by God, I ain't going to church anymore either, Jonah said to himself after he hung up the phone. Old God is going to have to leave me alone. Nobody went to church more than Ima. Well, hell *he* did too, smiling away and then the two of them kneeling next to one another at communion, God damn them both. Let the preacher go to Ninevah.

He hurried, combing his hair back, splashing cologne on, adjusting the white knit shirt at his neck so the sun wrinkles wouldn't show so much. He nearly killed himself cutting the stiff little whiskers in his nose. Whew! By God, though, he wasn't a bad looking man. Tall. Had a way with women still you betcha. By God, two could play at the musical chairs thing. And he had $120 and a good time would be had by Jonah Stark down there. That Duluth is always full of women hanging around places evenings—lonely women with that lonely look. Two women to every man down there. Don't need a lot of talk, most of them. Don't nag like Ima, whining, "Why dontcha talk to me, talk to me, talk to me...."

His Ford pickup started on the first turn of the key—a faithful beast it was with a camper in back and a 302 V-8. One of Ima's damn combs on the seat. He tossed it out. Or tried to. The damn window wasn't open. Plap! Cranked it open. Tossed it out on the lawn.

Slammed the pickup into gear, backed it up (over some of her roses), wheeled it down the driveway and aimed it down the curving, pine-edged dipping monotony of Highway 61 south to Duluth.

When he met the pastor's car coming up 61 he swore. "Go talk to her!" he yelled. "She's the one, not me!"

By God it wasn't so bad herding the pickup toward town with $120 in your pocket—some of her beauty shop money. That was good; that was good. Saturday night was when they did it while he was sitting in the Food-N-Fuel like a damn fool because there was no other work. It was high school girl's work sitting there, not fit for a real man.

At Two Harbors there is a theater—the only one in Lake County. They had sat in the show there together, he and Ima...saw a couple of good pictures. Lots of times he sat with his hand between her knees while she ate buttered popcorn...chewing away, smiling. A little nervous, not much.

The pain opened wide like an old cut splitting open inside him. He bent over a little and tried to force it shut.

How did it look when the two of them did it? The son-of-a-bitch, they played basketball together in high school. They never screwed anyone in high school. Nobody much did, he knew of. Well, there was.... Ima was pretty—the prettiest....

He fought a whimper—like the voice of a little boy inside him.

He wondered if the pastor was coming after him. Well, he wouldn't come into the place he was going to.

He wished someone would touch his head gently like his mother did.

He wished he was dead and buried. You don't think of anything then. Dead as a stone.

He had heard of this place once from some lumberjacks he worked with north of Hovland cutting cedar—nice, sweet-smelling cedar. Sometimes when he cut a tree—an old one—he felt a grief. Aaah—the tree cried, falling. Then the stump was just sitting there silent—a cut-down thing like an old man.

On Superior Street the place was—East Superior—down in the lower part of the city below the lights of the houses on the hills. In those houses maybe there were people who were good to one another, who knows.

There was a lot of street construction on Superior so it was hard to find the place, but then, just when he thought he was lost for sure, there it was waiting for him. He sat for a minute in the pickup and looked at it. The Black Finn it was called—a low, dark little place riding on pilings over murky waves on the big lake—riding so low, its shiplap belly seemed like it was in the water.

He wondered if he should go in there. The entrance was a red door shaped like an arched church window. On each side of it a lamp blinked yellow light.

So. Everywhere around him there were pickup trucks parked, their stiff rumps tilted up.

So.

Well, so he had to give it a try.

He looked at the Black Finn again. Its body extended over the water—a long one—blackened by weathering. Beached. There was a pretty tough crowd inside. You could hear their laughter ripple through the walls. He stuck a big crescent wrench into his belt under his sportcoat. He got out and approached the entrance. It was very dark—a kind of dark that can swallow a man—a cave dark. But he pushed forward and through the doors.

Inside the place he was talking to himself as he stood trying to adjust his eyes to the darkness. "By God, I don't know," he was saying. "This don't look right. This don't look friendly at all."

A man's swart round face appeared out of the scuffle of people at the bar. He stood in front of Jonah—close—too close. His breath was rank with onions. Jonah touched the wrench. The man reached for the wrench and held it and Jonah's hand in an iron grip; his arms were thick as cedar poles. "Oh, no you don't," he said. "We don't want any trouble with anyone."

"I don't want nobody giving me trouble," Jonah said. "I ain't even been drinking, but I'm alone."

"Well, you got a look of trouble about you. I'll take this nice thing. You sit over there at that table and you won't be alone for long. But no crazy business. I keep this place in order, do you understand?"

"Sure. So long as nobody tries anything with me."

"Well, they aren't going to hurt you."

"Who are you?"

"I'm the proprietor and the bouncer."

"I'm a jack," Jonah said. "I'm the only broadax man left in Cook County."

"Well you relax and have a good time. I've heard about you. Aren't you from up around Grand Marais?"

"Odin," Jonah said.

"Oh, yes. Odin. Well, no need to have a wrench or anything. No fighting here."

Jonah sat down then at a table on which many people had carved their initials sometime in the past. He sat, his back to the timber-ribbed wall. The wall seemed to move ever-so-slightly with some breath or sea motion or dark pulse. He looked at the crowd. Their faces were masks above the candles at the tables—smiling masks—masks leering with knowing things he did not know. They were moving all the time, the faces were, above a commotion of bodies and mouths, drinking. No one was leaving, but everyone seemed to be in a desperate hurry. The whole place was a belly full of people fleeing things.

He began to feel self-conscious and tired. He checked his billfold to see if it was there.

She. Round face. Fleshy arms on the table. Bosomed strong. Appeared in the captain's chair at his left.

"I said to myself such a handsome man should have some company," she said, smiling and touching his arm.

"Who are you?"

"Donya."

"From hereabouts?"

"Of course."

He fell silent because he didn't know what to say next.

"Do you want me to go?"

He looked at her face. She lolled her tongue over her upper lip. Her eyes were dark and soft in the candlelight.

"No, I don't want you to go."

"Well, you could buy me a drink. I'd like an old-fashioned."

"Old-fashioned what?" he asked, his face flushing because he knew it was stupid to ask that. He didn't drink much.

"Oh, everything," she said. "I'm really an old-fashioned girl."

"Well," he said, "we'll have what we want."

"That's nice."

He realized then, looking into his billfold for money, that he had his wedding ring on and he tried to cover it up by keeping his right hand on top of the table. He dropped his billfold and change.

"Don't cover it up," she said.

"I'm not doing so well," he said. "I'm too nervous. You see she cheated on me and I can't get used to it so I am very clumsy these days. I am not usually clumsy because I am a broadax man."

"A what?"

After the drinks came he explained to her. "I can square a log so it looks almost like a saw done it. I done an old church like that—a historical one."

She took his hand. "That is a good hand," she said.

His face flushed when she put a warm bare foot up into his crotch.

"I'll bet that's a good foot," she said.

"Almost," he said.

They had a couple more drinks. They seemed to exist in a little region of flickering candlelight.

"I sure do want to—to be with you close!" he said, blushing.

"Well, but you won't rush off afterward, will you?" she asked. Her face was serious and she held his hand under hers.

"I don't want to talk about it."

"All right, but you mustn't rush off afterward because I can't stand that."

"Me neither."

"You're not in trouble, are you?"

"No," he said hoarsely and loudly. "I ain't in any trouble. I ain't runnin' away from anything."

Suddenly, the floor of the place began to heave. Timbers creaked noisily and electric lanterns swung crazily on the walls. The lights dimmed, flickered, came on fully again.

"It's a storm," she said, holding his left hand in both of her hands. "It scares me here over the water."

To his left three men seemed to look at him, their playing cards held up in their hands like little fans.

He could swear they were all looking at him.

Thunder cracked and the Black Finn rocked on the waters surging and hissing beneath it.

"They built this for sea people," she said. "It won't break."

"I don't know," he said. He stared back at the three men and they dropped their eyes.

"I have a trailer house close by," she said. "It's pretty nice. Shall we?"

"It's raining so we'd better hurry," he said, his heart sticking in his throat.

"I don't want to be left alone," she said.

"You won't. I don't either. I promise I'll stay around a while tomorrow too."

As they passed the bouncer, Jonah said, "You keep the wrench. I don't need it. You got a good place here."

The bouncer said nothing. He nodded at Jonah, his eyes studying the two of them. His face was round and scarred like a moon. It had been hit many times.

In her trailer house there was the smell of the big lake. After they bathed together they stood up and let a lace curtain floating off a window caress them. She was dark and stout but solid, her thighs round, her stomach flat, her feet fine and tapered. The curtain caressed them together. Then she fell backward under him and he rode on her in long waves of desire.

When he awoke she was gone and that distressed him. He startled. What about his billfold? But it was all there—all of his money. The house trailer was very neat and clean. There was nothing on the walls except a little oval picture of a child with protuberant teeth and weepy eyes.

He felt depressed. He pulled his trousers on and stepped out of the trailer. The Black Finn would be a block away on the other side of it out of sight. A gray beach pebbled with purple-gray stone lay alongside the trailer. He walked out on it, coughing his usual morning cough. The sun was very bright.

Suddenly she was standing beside him in a wide-flowing white cotton dress. She took his arm and held it against a breast as he looked across the water.

"I've seen men like you before," she said.

"Oh? Other men. Well...."

"I mean that I've seen other men with that look you have."

"Maybe I really shot somebody or something," he said.

"No, you're running away from something else—nothing like that."

High on the hills above Duluth a church bell rang. He shivered under her touch.

"He's after me," he said, pushing her arm away and walking toward the water.

"He?"

"Yup. Thinks I should be someplace else."

She walked up to him and kissed his cheek lightly. "Me too," she said.

"What do you mean by that?"

"I mean somebody who thinks you've got to do something or not do it is after us."

"A pastor?"

"Or a priest. Or just a face or maybe a place where something was done or not done."

He nodded.

"Well, in the meantime...." she said.

"You're a smart woman," he said. "You've got wisdom like I've never seen before."

"Well, come inside now. I've got muffins," she said, "and then I can lie and talk with you...you need to lie with me, you know—just lie with me. Then you may be ready for new things—or old things."

"I guess so," he said. He was letting her lead him quietly into the shade inside the trailer where there were muffins and coffee cups and where there was her bed. She ran her hand over his shoulder and felt his body relax.

"You have good shoulders," she said, "and your eyes are good, too. You have a mother's eyes, you see. Don't you see that?"

"I ain't no mother," he said.

"I mean a woman likes a little bit of a mother in a man."

"That don't make sense to me," he said.

"You looked stricken when the bells rang," she said. "What joy is that?" The breeze fluttered her dress up over her knees. Her knees were waterlike and blue as she stood there.

"I ain't sure," he said. "Maybe he himself ain't much for joy."

"Come and take some cakes and coffee and then lie with me awhile...."

"I can't promise much. It might be hard to get away again," he said.

"That's all right," she said. "This time is as good as any."

"You see," he said, "they always manage to find you again. It's just about impossible to get away from it all."

"Shhhhh!" she whispered. "You come and be with me. We'll be good to each other in little ways."

A Bear and a Kiss

As he drove the new Ford pickup deeper into hazy gray-green stands of pine and fir, Jaeger wondered whether he was going to the hunting camp to fill some deep void in himself or to somehow empty something out of himself. It was always that way when he went hunting—first brimming excitement, then, when he got there—when he stood in the deep cathedral places in the pine stands—something else—a slow, sad pulse—something—something lately.

And so he brought the boy with him—the kid, yes the kid. He was seventeen and he was sleeping on the seat next to Jaeger. His face looked adenoidal and wan and babyish as it usually did when the kid was exhausted. Jaeger had picked him up at the Amoco station when he came off a graveyard shift as cashier. Before that, in spite of his father's warning about the need to be on his toes hunting, he had run all over town with his restless buddies. No use to talk to any of them. They all think they're immortal—drive that way; run that way. And, of course, Jaeger had to do all of the preparation for the trip himself.

So not much conversation going on. And on the radio nothing but country western music and all kinds of local ads by small town radio announcers gifted at hype. "You'll find the folks at Nelson's Furniture ready to help you find the bed or sofa or table just right for you!" one of them was crying. Sure.

So Jaeger looked at the woods. What's it all really good for? he asked himself half-kidding. There's so damn much of them. You'd like to do something to them—what, you're not sure—but they always manage to wear you out—to do something to you somehow. Look back. There they are, nodding and you going by and knowing things.

The kid groaned, pitched over and tried to pull his knees up. No luck. And what a hard-on the kid had. Well, good for him. Kids sure get a lot more of everything these days. Jaeger was a virgin at twenty-five—no fault of his own. But then Japan on R & R...ah!

Seventy miles farther up Highway 61 Jaeger decided (what the hell!) he wanted to do two things up north: to kill a bear with his bow; and to kiss a Finnish girl—a young woman—in or near Finnmark—a ragged little ethnic town cut into the woods by Finnish settlers a hundred years back. Of course, the kid was with him.... So it wasn't logical! It still made sense though, somehow.

The bugs were bad. Jaeger winced when heavy beetles and moths hit the windshield and grill. Got to wash them off right away, he mused. Acid goes right through the paint. Leaves pits.

To his right as he slowed into a little two-store village, a girl was mowing a lawn with a riding tractor—mowing right up to the highway. Long legs, tight mane of yellow hair, pursed mouth. Her knees levered up around the steering wheel; the levers moved between her legs; then, with an insolent roar, tractor and girl receded southward behind the pickup and Jaeger shook his head to get rid of a flash of sadness.

Finnmark was just around the next curve. No it wasn't. Damn curves all looked alike. It made him crabby to think of it.

"Jeez! Put some music on!"

It was the kid coming out of sleep—apparently nice sleep. They even have better dreams at his age.

"Nothin' on!" Jaeger said, "—except *hard country!*"

But the kid turned the damn thing on anyway. Jaeger wouldn't let him take the little stereo cassette with the headphones like he had the last time. Let a bear crash through the brush fifty feet behind him while he was off somewhere with Bruce Springsteen.

He turned the Duluth station on *loud.*

"Loud is good! Right?" Jaeger yelled.

"Right!"

Now, thought Jaeger, he'll want to eat. He isn't really in the spirit of the thing with me, is he? Electronic search—that's his sport.

"When do we stop to eat?"

"After we get there."

"Jeez! I'm hungry, Dad!"

"Ten minutes!" Jaeger yelled. "I want to get some hunting in!"

In eight minutes (Jaeger was nervous—they had just the evening and morning—he wanted the kid to have a good time—he kept checking his watch and driving faster) they rolled into Finnmark and then down a narrow winding road. The trees were very close to the road and their limbs scratched at the side of the pickup, squealing, screeching gleefully. Jaeger winced and swore.

"They won't hurt it!" the kid yelled, sulking in his collar.

"It's scratching the hell out of it!"

"No it's not."

"Turn it *down*!"

Then Jaeger said, trying to be conciliatory, "When I lived in Odin I used to date girls over here."

No reply.

At the end of the road—deep in what looked like a cave of darkness in the trees—was the Maki Resort, a little crescent of unpainted fishing and hunting shacks, hunched moss-backed and brown on the edge of the lake. In the center of the crescent of shacks was a new one—rough-sawn vertical pine and wood-shingle roof. That was the Maki home and the office and the breakfast cafe. Funny people—taciturn, odd people with severe blue eyes. Somebody said the Finns inbred too much and that was why there were strange repeated facial oddities and hearing defects that put hearing aids on the little kids.

Except for the girl. She was something else. Jaeger had watched her grow up—season after season—with the fishing and the hunting. The kid and she had run like cubs down along the lake the first time they saw each other.... A taste of honey.... They were together for two weeks—sunning, running....

"Why don't we stay in Duluth and drive out? Or in Odin?" the kid asked breaking into Jaeger's reverie.

"It takes too much time."

"Jeez! We've got so much time we don't know what to do with it...."

"You got to be patient if you're a hunter."

The pickup was stopped. Jaeger could smell the hot bugs on the radiator. "Come on!" he said to the kid, punching his knee easily. The kid hit back vaguely. But he got out anyway.

The old Finn—the grandfather—trollish and ragged and sharp-faced as a sparrow—checked them in, writing "Jaeger and Boy" on a slate with chalk. He was a laconic man except when it came to talking to himself.

When the old man cleared his throat, Jaeger put his hand on the kid's shoulder to get him to pay attention.

"Well, now," the old Finn said, not even bothering to gesture, "you go west of here along the old lumber trail and you'll see something if you are patient."

That was it. The words of wisdom. The old Finn disappeared into the kitchen. The kid had turned away with that damn schoolboy smirk on his face and was outside, framed in the doorway....

...talking to the girl—Sunny. She was seventeen or so. How could the kid be so nonchalant while she stood there in that very little swim suit—a blue-eyed angel with just the right amount of woman flesh on her—curved, delicious belly, pert breasts, fine legs. She had none of the peculiarities the others had. She had a natural grace about her. She was bound for college somewhere. She was lovely in a sweet, unself-conscious way. High, smooth cheeks, honey-tanned, berry-mouthed.

Stop it, he told himself.

She made Jaeger sad, the way the tall suppleness of the birches and other things did lately.

When the girl turned to go away, she snapped the edge of her swim suit over one of the moons of her ass. Jaeger took a quick breath. The kid didn't even notice. I hope I never get *that* tired, Jaeger told himself. It was a bad joke.

It was just then that Jaeger noticed the old Finn was standing by the vaporous hissing of the aerated live bait tank where minnows and frogs were kept.

"So you think we'll find a bear?" Jaeger asked, dropping his eyes to avert the old man's very blue ones.

"Bears like sweet things," he said. Jaeger nodded and the old man went on. "It is sad when old bears like sweet things and they are too high on the tree and such things. I have heard gray-furred old ones cry at such times." Jaeger nodded. "Of course, in the morning there are often bears by the garbage pit down the road that bends off the lumber trail. But those are not good bears and it is not a sporting thing to shoot one in a place where the bear is not a creature of the wilderness. It is not a clean good hunt then." Jaeger nodded. "But some do it anyway—desperate ones!" He was shaking his head sadly. Jaeger nodded and the old Finn disappeared again—without another word.

They hunted with bows and arrows—his son and he. They had practiced through much of the summer and early fall at a range at a sportsmen's club in St. Paul. The bows were powerful steel ones that looked like refined old automobile leaf springs and shot arrows so swiftly you would hardly see them until—zick!—one appeared on the face of the target like a ray of green or silver light suddenly visible and solid.

They saw nothing that first evening of the hunt. The kid was brooding, his collar up around his neck. It rained a little. Trees dripped. Jaeger felt responsible for the rain. He was a caretaker. He felt responsible for everything. The odor of decaying vegetation and the ruins of fallen bodies of trees were rich and rank in the rain.

The two of them—he and the kid—ate dinner in Odin. The Maki Resort served only breakfast. There was hardly a soul in town. Bow hunting was a special season that didn't attract so many hunters. The kid played the jukebox, ate everything including an extra malted milk, leaned way back into the varnished brown booth, lolled his eyes and listened to the screeching of some rock group named after a dirigible. The stars were out as they stepped outside into the street.

"The hunter is up there!" he said, pointing to Orion.

"Sure, Dad!"

"You're not a stargazer."

"What?"

"You know—with a girl or something. You just watch TV with them."

"I'm tired," he said. "I don't know what you mean."

They drove back to the hunting shack in silence—except for the radio.

Can men make friends—even with their own sons? Jaeger wondered.

During the night the kid got up and fished through Jaeger's clothes and took out the keys to the pickup. So, what could Jaeger say to him after the rain and the bad hunt? In the orange light from the oil stove that was flickering and sputtering in the corner of the shack the kid's face looked like many of those hyped orange faces in videos on TV. What was the look? Smug? Lusty? Joyful?

By the time Jaeger thought through the question and the speculation, the kid was gone and Jaeger was left to worry about the extra scratches on the pickup. Then he couldn't sleep. He got up after a while and looked out and saw the old Finn standing out there looking down the road where the two of them had driven off. The furred limbs of the trees made the road a dark tunnel under the stars. Jaeger coughed and crawled back in bed.

In the morning the kid was hard to wake up. He was also hard.

"What's the hurry!" he groaned. "There's nothin' out there." Lying there, he had a look of satisfaction about him.

For just a second, Jaeger hated that look. Then he was mad. "Get yours out of bed and get goin'!" he yelled.

"All right! All right!" the kid complained.

After he asked it—at breakfast in the back of the main lodge—the grandfather serving half a dozen sullen, brooding hunters, including one gaunt and gray old man who stared constantly at the window facing the woods—Jaeger wished he hadn't.

"How was it?" he asked in a whisper. That was what he and his buddies used to ask when they suspected. Jaeger got silent reproof—contempt by silence.

The old hunter was moaning at his coffee cup. His hands on the cup were blue as ice and, when he took them off the cup, they trembled slightly. The younger hunters weren't saying much—just muttering phrases about weather and bears—and women of course. Through the kitchen door Jaeger could see the girl at the big black stove. Looking a bit tired.

"Don't know as I can get up here again next year," the old hunter said.

"What?" Jaeger realized he was talking to him.

"I'm not supposed to be up here this year in fact," he continued. "But I want to get a bear. It's a silly notion, but then from here on in it's maybe playing pinochle and fishing on a bridge in the city with a lot of other old farts."

"I suppose," Jaeger said.

"It's Dad's last year too," the kid interjected.

Jaeger turned to look at him. "What the hell do you mean?" he asked.

"He's young. He thinks we're all old. Old is old," the old hunter said. "It just happens to you one day."

"Just kidding!" the kid said.

"So, where you hunting?" Jaeger asked, trying to change the subject.

"West of here."

"We'll be on the old lumber trail."

"I won't be there. I just sit someplace easy."

The old man's hands were trembling again—a low-frequency flutter like the wings of a stricken bird. His arms under the red and black flannel shirt were tissue and bone.

He was getting up. Flatulent.

"God!" he moaned. "I'm sorry about that!"

The kid had his face down in the pancakes. He cleared his throat and snickered.

"We're late!" Jaeger snapped. The others were all rising and heading out.

The kid shrugged his shoulders.

And then, when it was really too light for surprising a bear or hiding in a good position, the two of them were finally walking down the lumber road. The underbrush was wet and made Jaeger cough.

"Maybe you shouldn't do this!"

"Maybe you shouldn't do some things, yourself!" Jaeger said.

As they walked, they tried to carry the bows over their shoulders like rifles, but it was clumsy, very clumsy.

"What the hell is that?" the kid cried.

Jaeger stopped. Just down the garbage pit road to their left there was a pitiful crying—not human—but then human too—two voices.

"Jesus God!" the kid cried. "I can see them."

They moved closer.

Yes—them. The bear first—rolling in a convulsive fur ball, then rising, its paws tearing at the feather of an aluminum arrow in its guts. It was an old bear—one forced to rummage for trash in a garbage pit. It stood there, looking at Jaeger, beseeching him, then raging at him, until the pain made it turn its attention back on itself where the arrow ran sideways into its belly—its cavern of appetites.

Then Jaeger saw the old man—the one from breakfast—standing to the left. His hat had fallen off and was a queer orange patch at his feet. His head was bent over his bow. He was crying as he tried to string another arrow on the bow. The string made a weird little humming noise as it slipped out of his fingers. "Oh, dear God!" he cried again and again. "Have mercy! Have mercy on an old man!"

Jaeger could smell the rotting garbage in the wind through the trees. He moved towards the bear. There were streaks of silver on its head and snout. Something—garbage perhaps—was matted in its fur and, except for its distended belly, it was thin, emaciated-looking.

Jaeger strung his bow. The kid did too—quickly.

With a howl the bear rolled against a poplar tree, then suddenly stood up and began to run at Jaeger. The kid's arrow hit it then, bursting the heart so it spit blood as the bear ran a few steps more and fell softly, silently.

The old man sat on the ground and sobbed, unused arrows strewn on the ground all around him.

The kid had disappeared after shooting the bear.

In the warmth of the sun there was a sweet smell of old garbage and new blood. A fly—hideous little bat of blood—buzzed at the nostrils of the bear whose eyes regarded Jaeger with an anthracite blankness. The old man whimpered.

The kid's bow and arrow lay on the ground—the way his little plastic one had in the backyard a long time....

Jaeger had wanted him to have a good time.

The old man had stopped crying. When he spoke finally, his voice was hollow and plaintive. "I wanted a bear so bad!" he said. "I can't even get one in this kind of place. And I made the poor bastard suffer so!"

"Well, I wanted one too," Jaeger said.

The kid was packing the pickup when Jaeger got back to the shack. He wasn't saying anything, just carrying things—moving miraculously fast for a change. Jaeger shrugged his shoulders. "Sorry, kid!" he said. Then they worked together to get it all ready to go.

When they were sitting in the pickup, the old Finn came out. "You want a refund?" he asked up at them. Jaeger shook his head and the old man disappeared into one of the little shacks—to clean, to brood maybe.

The girl seemed to come out just when the sun burst over the trees. She wore a light blue skirt and a yellow blouse. There was a quiet rush of golden light with her.

She made Jaeger sad again. God she was beautiful. She stood there with her arms folded the way rural women do when men are doing things—things the women maybe have no say about. She was looking down and kicking at something when Jaeger heard the old man's cries getting closer.

"Come on, Dad! Let's get out of here. This is awful."

"Just a minute," Jaeger said. "I want to see about something. What are you so embarrassed about?"

"For shit's sake!" He did a little foot stomp on the floor of the pickup.

Jaeger swung the door open and stepped out. By God you just don't leave like this. You just don't drive off leaving a lot of chaos.

The girl was looking at him, her eyes full of worry and something else. The look of worry deepened when the old man's sounds rippled through the trees at the edge of the cabins.

She looked like she was going to cry.

"I could just die!" she said.

"Why?" he asked. "Why should you feel embarrassed because of what us older folks do?"

"I don't know—this old place is odd and just awful."

"It wasn't before the old man did his thing," Jaeger said, his voice dropping into a tone of paternal blessing—the reassuring voice he used with his kids when they were small and grieving.

He put his arm around her shoulder.

"I'm going to get out of here," she said, crying, her voice steady though.

"Why are you taking all of this on?" he asked. "It's one of those things that shouldn't have happened. Your grandfather warned us too. It's not his fault either."

"He just wants to go," she said—meaning the kid, he guessed.

"He's embarrassed too," Jaeger said. "You're both at the age when it's easy to be embarrassed."

He kissed her on the cheek and then (My God!) almost kissed her on the mouth. Her eyes widened at him and she stepped backward.

Behind him Jaeger could hear the stereo in the truck blaring so loudly the ground seemed to vibrate with the noise.

"Thank you," he said.

She stared at him.

"For just one nice moment," he said.

"Could I ride to town with you until it's over—with the bear I mean?"

"Sure," he said. "Come on. I'll let you two talk while I call home."

"Do you think he'll mind?"

"He'll pretend to but he won't really."

My God! The kid would hardly move so she could get into the pickup with them. He *wouldn't* let her sit between them.

"She's riding into town with us!" Jaeger yelled into the fury of the music. Then he got in.

As they rode toward town, Jaeger let the music blast away. It was a hard rock love song in which a yowling young voice claimed the capacity to make love all night. "Come on! Come on!" the voice kept crying. Well, it kept Jaeger from hearing the tree branches scratching at the side of the pickup. So let it all go on.

Beside him the kid and the girl weren't talking or quite touching. They just looked straight ahead like two frightened creatures.

Jaeger felt a perverse impulse to yell something himself. But what would it be?

The girl's legs were levered upward slightly so her lovely knees were dappled wonderfully by the shadows of the passing trees.

Jaeger drove fast, fighting back a huge smile.
What the hell! You win some; you lose some.

Misericorde

He knelt between her legs and discovered his own knees again after their cries and whispers. His knees were tingling with little needles of pain from the abrasive things on the rubber floormat of the car. Her tanned legs were spread widely, his pale hips between them. Behind him he saw the painted nails of her dark feet making red staccato notes on the dash and he frowned. They were done with lovemaking and he wanted to go back but she wasn't letting go. Her knees were two smooth knuckles and he was held between them.

"No, you don't," she said. She was smiling but serious, her dark hair flowing over him.

"It's coming out on the seat," he said. His voice was hoarse and he hated that because he felt weak and vulnerable.

There was a rustle of Kleenex and she pressed some of it around his flaccid penis, barely lifting him to do it. Then, with her mouth, she was demanding kisses—again and again—and it suddenly occurred to him that his mouth was sore and it would show—show puffiness, unusual redness—usage.

And even while dutifully kissing her he began to detach himself and to run somehow in his mind back to the parsonage on the hill to Katherine. His mouth made kissing noises; his voice said things. But he was already writhing inside his own body and the car. He wanted to go. He was done. The function was complete. He was done with this woman. He wished to be back with Katherine.

And Katherine would be there in the old sitting room of the parsonage.

She would be—nearly always—sitting at the ancient black Chickering grand piano they had brought with them from Massachusetts via Chicago. The piano was a heavy thing, a thing steady in the motion of his confusion.

Yes. Katherine at the piano always held her fine, long neck that way she had learned somewhere and the dress was a satin green and smooth with puffed sleeves and her hair was copper. A rose—fair—refined, rarefied: icon.

He felt his face turned to be kissed on the mouth by this other woman, to be pressed to moist attention to her mouth, and he opened his eyes to her dark eyes and hair again. Rain dark grass in the night of day. Her painted toenails on the dash, staccato. But no deep chords were playing for him.

Piano.

Has no body, Katherine. The piano does, but she herself had not quite a body.

A mouth pressed his, hard and flat. The wine maybe and that other taste as with copper if it were liquid. Spigot of her lower body—dark, forbidden wine, now dregs.

"I wanted to again," she cried.

"But you came."

"Yes, but...."

"Yes, you came and I did, but we are going nowhere."

"Don't say that. At least pretend with me or I'll feel even more rotten...."

"We've stretched our luck staying here this long," he complained, his body twisting out of its captivity. She loomed over him, bronzing in the light. A breast appeared at his mouth—plumlike and delicate. He took it for a moment with his mouth.

"You're not getting rid of me so easily, are you?" her voice said above him. Her dark hair fanned over his head like the top of a tree. He slipped away as plaintive notes—a motif—go back to an instrument, longing to be played again.

...the black piano is playing in the tall living room of the parsonage. She sits like an adolescent girl at a piano recital. What is he there? Teacher? No. He sits listening, a grim coldness in his crotch, and listens to the piece, "Widmung." A solemn oak clock is ticking through the music. Wooden are the days. Though it is summer the rays of sunlight in the room have the heft of cathedral light on winter afternoons. They are so ponderous they assume volume and substance and finality....

"What's that?" A voice through the bones of his head—this other woman's—.

He could hear a howling and snarling behind them on the trail they had taken into the woods. They had driven a long way in—he worrying and she laughing, her mouth at his ear.

"What is it?" she asked, whispering.

"A chain saw," he said.

He found himself in a scuffle of legs and clothes. Then they were sitting up together, alert and formal, two hearts beating tremors of alarm. Sitting as stiffly as they might on a church bench.

"See," he said, itching his beard and looking cautiously into the rearview mirror. "I've tried to tell you we shouldn't stay in one place too long."

"As long as it's long enough for you of course."

"Come on, now."

His heart was hammering as the chain saw started again, muttered, growled and then howled into wood.

"Oh, dear God! I'll be so late!" he said. A dagger seemed to pierce his chest.

"Don't you think I will?"

They were sitting apart as if someone were watching.

He tied his tie and adjusted his clothes. She adjusted her clothes too, a curious bulge in the crotch of her jeans where the wad of Kleenex was. Her blouse was purple and her eyes dark—a French genealogy with the history of the county in the north woods—voyageurs maybe—she an exotic—a dark figure vibrant with passion. She was hard to satisfy because of her hungry self. She was one who could not quite ever endure the common good of life....

"We could be cut off," he said.

"I hope not," she said putting her hand on his crotch and forcing another nervous smile.

"Could you walk from here?"

"Are you serious? I haven't got the shoes for it."

"Couldn't you cut through the woods?"

"I haven't got the shoes, I said."

"Well, we may be caught, then...."

Ebony piano notes far off, a faded rose the player. Then a dissonance of keys played too fast.

"They're cutting down trees. We'll be discovered for sure."

Behind them on the road a tree aw-awed and its body crashed down into underbrush.

"There are risks in these things, Mr. Dimmesdale."

"What? That's not funny at all."

"I could duck down."

"Not yet. If they're watching, that'll be a dead giveaway."

"I've ducked down a lot," she said, "—a dozen times my head on your lap. But truckers could see me from their cabs. Somebody always sees you."

"Be ready," he said, his heart thumping. As he began to back down the winding trail leading to the main road, the limbs of the pines and aspens ran on the car.

Then, when the car reached a turn in the trail, he cried out. A freshly-cut jack pine lay across the trail, its stump white and splintered and raw. It was a good-sized tree—too heavy to move by hand. It lay there heavily—a ponderous sudden barrier.

"Oh, Christ!" she cried. "Where are they?"

He turned the motor off and listened. She was crouching down in the seat, her eyes animal-crazy with fear.

There was no one in sight and no way of seeing anyone in the thick brush along the edges anyway. He opened the car window. Silence—except for the wind soughing in the tops of the trees, and far off in the distance, the cawing of crows.

There on a prominent branch bending down toward them was pinned something.

"Don't go out there. It could be my husband."

"I've got to."

He stepped out of the car and approached the note and the fallen tree. The note was scribbled on yellow paper:

> UNITARIAN
> You make yourself a *good*
> fellow by preaching there's
> no sin. You sin. Here is
> an ax. Think.

He looked around again. No one. But there, its yellow ash handle leaning against the trunk of the tree, was the ax. He took it and the note and walked back toward the car, her bright and frightened eyes on him all the time.

"They've been here," he said, handing her the note.

"Who?"

"The elders. The ones who watch you."

She stiffened out in the car seat and threw a quick twisting tantrum. "Oh, why?" she cried before she slumped back down in the seat, depressed and rigid.

"I have to cut us out," he said, noting, she doesn't even wonder about the ax. She never wondered about such things. "I'm not good with one of these," he added.

She was saying nothing. Well, what could she say? Not much grace under pressure. But then someone might be watching. She was done with him too and wanted to be back in the rambler where her husband babysat with her children. Of course, in between, he would have to drop her off by her car up another pine-winy old lumber trail two miles away.

He removed his suit coat and began to work. It was hard—very hard. He discovered he had not cut a wide enough wedge the first time and had to open the cut wider so the ax was not coming down vertically on the cross grain. It took, it seemed, forever. And every blow seemed to echo loudly through infinities of woods. She sat there profoundly depressed, limp, dark-eyed with vague doom. Well, good. He cut branches, threw them aside.

Finally, he could see that there was room for his car to pass. He stopped, put the ax carefully back where he found it. He thought about writing a note himself but knew that was foolish. Don't lie. Just don't say anything. That was her motto too.

As they drove out, she threw her head back and began to cry. Often she cried when they made love. She had a kind of adoration for him— the preacher—a man with power over people from birth to death. Yes.

He drove up the road where she had left her car. It was there, shining blue through the trees. She sprang out of his car, crying, "I'm not letting you go! I want to see you again!" He drove off without even waiting to see if her car started. But then, behind him, he saw her coming and she passed him without looking as she entered the town, speeding past the 30 mph sign.

...where do you enter a rose to love it? A rose, sitting at a black piano is love and plays love. Yes, but that doesn't work...the body...she does not quite have a body though she has legs, breasts...if you look far enough you will see that there is only a blank mannequin aridity between her legs, though a rose, of course, has no legs...what has she done with it in the two years in the tall-roomed parsonage....? If only, after the child-death, she had not put her own body away. And she lives in the piano that is her only body.

The first time that she—the dark Esther—came to see him, to be counseled, she sat there with her skirt hiking up her legs with each exclamation of frustration with her life. "Is this all there is?" she kept asking. "No," he wanted to say, "I hope not—not for so much beauty!" Then he said it and she looked at him and pressed her hand on his and he was immediately aroused. The wonder of her thighs—the marvelous mystery of the distance between liquid knee and pubic meadow—caught his fancy and he could think of nothing except that aching, terrible distance. Nights ached in his head as he lay with Katherine. Katherine lay asleep, hearing music in some far-off dark corridor, her own dark body downstairs, silent in the parlor, under the black piano lid.

Driving along the country roads he wished to be enclosed with something—covered—protected from eyes. Who were the men in the woods? His own parishioners? What could he explain to anyone? The facile cliche: I made a mistake and forgot the advice they gave us in seminary. Don't touch such a woman unless your wife is present. Even then...this Esther was vulnerable, not having been touched for so long she couldn't remember the last time. When touched by Peabody she whimpered and opened like a flower to the sun so he fell from the sky on her—swanlike, his thighs beating.

He drove quickly toward the town and then, on the edge of it just past the Lutheran church, toward her home to see what he could see. He had done it before. This time he knew how to look without appearing to look. The key was to size up everything from a distance. He swung the car onto the winding street and held it steady at thirty. A block away he saw her car parked in the driveway. Beyond it, the blue and purple flag of her jeans and blouse moved among children playing on little nervous tricycles. There, at the great yawning gate of the church cemetery, he prepared himself to drive past. Who might be there? The choppers?

Her husband. The car nearly hit him when he stepped out on the road to turn the lawn mower around. He was looking at Peabody, the eyes calm with the old tragedy of betrayal. Peabody's eyes did not meet his. He waved and drove by for the last time. In the mirror he felt the man's eyes following him.

It was all perilous passage.

To get to his own church and parsonage he would also have to pass the slough. It was a vast region of shallow water bordered by tall grass at the south end of the lake. He stopped the car again. Opened the window. The grass waved at him, beckoned him, calling to him with long, undulating whispers. On a winter evening, under the first stars, he had sat in the car after seeing her and had felt the blue infinity of ice and snow beyond the grass...and was comforted by its amazing familiarity. The north is of the soul, not of the map. Dissolution into blue and evanescent distances. But the cold, the cold light.

He drove on, listening to the dust ticking and buzzing under the car as it whirled out behind him. He was hearing the throb of old music inside himself again. From where? It, too, had a familiarity—fugal—from some antiquity. What the heart, the hand, that made it? Not blue or green was it, but purple and in his blood, beating.

His church rose up through the pines on his right—white, erect—a New England church on a New England hill in the north country of Minnesota. A kind of historical accident it was. The Lutherans could not decide among themselves where to build—on the hill or there by the cemetery on the west edge of the town. Then the Unitarian divine from Chicago spoke to those who wanted the church on the hill. He offered them part of the dream of the city on the hill and release from the tedious doctrine of original sin and the oppressiveness of creed and strict doctrine. In one afternoon he made one hundred twenty-five converts and established this, the first Unitarian church in rural Minnesota. The Lutherans who were left behind built their own church of stone, not clapboard. On Sunday the German hymns hung heavily on the air while Peabody, tall in the pulpit, attacked the words in the Lutheran liturgy: "I believe that I am by nature sinful and unclean." He preached a simple doctrine: God loves you and so do I. It made him feel good—especially when parishioners from the Lutheran church came to him for comfort. But did he give it?

And *she* came and he comforted her and then, when she opened to him he entered her and was himself comforted for brief moments. But after passion a formal feeling comes.

Of late she became complicated—too complicated—a woman asking theological questions. "If there's no sin what will become of us?" she asked. "What do we do about all the people we've hurt and what do they do about us? And who is bigger than us with a heart so big that somehow we cannot hate each other forever?"

His ancestors might have hanged her for a witch.

"That's not what it's all about," he would say.

"You're being patronizing," she would say.

And yet they met to do it—in some dim dale in the woods beyond the clearing, in what Hawthorne—Peabody's ancestor by marriage—saw as the place of revelation of the spirit within oneself.

A car met him.

He waved, but the man did not wave back.

Dear God, surely they knew—all of them. He was sure of it. There could've been a dozen of them.

The quick birds of gossip were sitting at all the edges of his world and flying off on black wings of rumor.

They knew—all of them.

He wished to be somewhere at such a depth that no one could find him. Not in the grass of a slough where one could be found like a pathetic, croaking frog. Deeper. Deeper.

He turned the car into the tarred road running up to the church—up past the gazebo and the well.

The well. Wellness.

The spire. Piercing—a dagger. A visual scream.

He stopped the car in the shadow of the steeple. Dizzy he was and confused.

Henry Pierson, the grounds keeper, was cleaning out the fern bed by the foundation of the church, kneeling there; tearing the weeds out; beating the earth out of the roots with large brown hands.

I shall find a solace there....

Someone had him by the elbow. He had himself by the elbow. He pushed himself out of the car.

"Hello, Henry," he said.

No answer—only a flurry of digging.

Well, he said to himself, perhaps the dead will answer or listen. He walked up through the gate and into the cemetery.

Is this all there is? Why hadn't Katherine and he gone away?

There at his feet was their daughter Sophia's grave. Where else could they have gone after her death? How could they leave it behind? Even dying she had been abandoned by both of them. She was nine. Cancer. She fought. She had an old face—a brown chemical face as from a photo made in another time. She was angry at the cancer for entering her body in such a way. She screamed and raged. Her mind was fine—a silver note in a dying light. He preached at her funeral: "Wear Your Tribulation Like a Rose."

He tried to breathe deeply but couldn't. The wind breathed deeply through the pines. Symbols of eternal life. Ha! Under them dust off the fields. She loved him. That is why she raged at going. Her mother sat by the bed—silent. The piano was her only voice for many things.

Is dust our pilgrimage?

Who knows our suffering?

Who suffers to know us?

He turned, tired of it, his head throbbing, and approached the parsonage, preparing his words: We will have to get counseling to help us see the meaning of our lives. Katherine? Did you hear me? We can go to Duluth. This is a pretty enlightened congregation. We may be able to stick it out.

A dry, disembodied voice merely says, "Some suffering cancels all we know of meaning."

He entered the front door of the parsonage instead of going though the kitchen as he usually did. For a moment he saw himself in the vertical oval glass of the door. A long face, bespectacled, an Emersonian nose, shifting blue eyes.

Oh, anyone seeing that face would know. He opened the door quietly and entered the room with soft steps.

She sat at the piano but was not really sitting at the piano because there was only a rose there—a rose without voice. The thorns of silence rejected his words and touch. If the rose had turned toward him, its petaled mouth would only have accused him.

There was nothing to say to it.

He turned and went up the stairs to the bathroom. There he removed two bottles of aspirin from the medicine cabinet. He poured himself a large glass of water and took them all. In the mirror he saw himself gorging them down, his face bestial with mad appetite.

He hurried downstairs and then out on the lawn. The grounds keeper had left. Behind him, no music. Beyond the churchyard the open spaces that would reveal him. And in a closed room somewhere during the next days, there would be humiliation and indignity with the deacons. He must do to himself, for himself. The best way. Self-reliance. Every heart vibrates to that iron string.

He walked to the well and stood there. His body was already cooling down and the aspirin taking effect. Too late. Sometimes it is too late. His stomach ached; his knees were shaking weakly.

He lifted the wooden cover from the well, mounted the stone edge, suffered, heard no voices, and stepped out into cold darkness where he could not take a breath at all. In an oozy dream for one moment he cried out like a child and a great heart, as of a sea, beat once with his....

......

Esther stood inside the garage, her heart pounding, her car keys in hand, poised like a frightened bird ready for flight without direction. She was held there by words spoken in the hollow wooden cavern of the garage next door where the neighbors were discussing it—the news. She could not hear it all, only enough.

"Jumped in the well feet first."

"Dear God!"

"Well, I'll tell you they had a hard time getting him out."

"What do you mean?"

"He was *standing* in there."

"So?"

"They couldn't get at him. I mean they couldn't get at his feet or arms with the rope."

"Oh, my God!"

"So they had to pull him up by the neck."

"Oh, my God!"

"One old farmer asked, 'Is he dead?' and another said, 'Well, if he wasn't down there he got that way being pulled up, I suppose,' and another said, 'Odin.'"

"Odin."

"Yes."

"I don't get it."

A laugh, flat and without feeling.

"No one knows why."

"Somebody does, but they're not saying."

Esther started toward the car, travel case hanging a long way off on her left hand, but her husband caught her and held her in his arms and they stood there while the unrelenting voices went on. His heart was beating fiercely against her.

"His wife has been sickly but she just seemed to wake up and take care of things out there. Didn't cry at all. Just walked out of the parsonage and took charge of things. You have to respect her for that—a skinny, nervous little woman like that. Hardly anything to her, but she took hold."

Esther dropped the travel case and began to cry. Her husband picked it up and led her into the kitchen and made her a good, stiff drink and she threw the car keys back into the drawer by the sink and began to talk about making dinner for the kids, who would be coming in from playing outside. Even while she talked about the food he held her close. His heart was pulsating; she could feel it through her blouse. She let him hold her a long time. And then they moved apart when the children burst into the kitchen and she turned and began to take things out of the refrigerator.

Two: A Story of Numbers

Hunkering under the wind and snow in his duck boat, Dr. Liv wonders why he is there. He is one of two dentists in Odin—the one with the funny name. In Norwegian it means life, but today Dr. Liv is at the business of killing, and the irony of it tickles him a little under the numbing cold. The gray water beats through the buzz and hum of the bending reeds and rocks him slowly. Twenty yards out on the open water his decoys, plastic on the waves, bob up and down and tug at their anchor strings. Farther out on the snow-veiled, sullen expanses of Heron Lake long traceries of migrating scaup vortex down to rest on the water and then to fly again. They know. In the morning the wind will be still, the land snow-burdened and the lake an eye of blue ice—except in the very middle where a few birds will linger—hurt or crazy or whatever they are.

Wet snow drips from Liv's enormous ruddy nose. To keep warm, he hugs himself, looking down occasionally at the thin gunwale that separates him from the rages of water. Under the surface there are fields of silt four or five feet deep—silt oozed from the farm fields through creek and tile pipe. He shudders and thinks of going home. Men have been found standing up in the lake, the silt up to their necks—one with his gun still across his arms. Hunting still.

The white bellies of the mallards flash in the corner of his eye and pass behind him. Turning is a stiff and clumsy thing for Liv, so he lets them circle. The two of them hang on the wind above him, their wings moving slowly. A pair of curly tails they are—a drake and hen—from Hudson Bay or God-only-knows-where—a far north anyway. And wheat-fat they are too.

Liv is amazed to see them swing and drop into the shallow water closer to the shore. They begin to feed, paddling and then tilting their bottoms up like sails of distant sailboats. He yells to flush them and they rise nearly straight up, their wings flailing. Liv aims at the drake's head. The shot punches them and they both fall, one plummeting; the other flapping down sideways to splash in the weeds.

"Damn it!" Liv cries. The limit is one mallard and one of them is wounded. He rows madly towards them. A wounded mallard is crazy— a cunning diver—like shooting a submarine.

He sees that the drake is near death and is pulsing around and around in a savage convulsive circle. The hen swims away, only her periscoped head showing. Damn her!

And Liv paddles, hurtling toward her, pausing to shoot, paddling, pausing to shoot. Until, finally, she is flapping wildly on the surface, then lying still on one side, her gleaming eye accusing him through the gray-green froth. Liv picks her up and slides her over the gunwale.

It will be necessary to make an extra trip to town to get rid of the second bird. He cannot take a chance on getting caught with two birds. Yes, the possession limit is two, but one must be cold. They insert a little thermometer into them to see if they are warm or cold. The drake is caught in the weeds. He floats on his belly so his form is long and dark. The hen he has in hand—dun, long and graceful she is—and delicate her orange feet and steady her brown-glass eye.

When Liv pulls his boat on shore he sees the sheet of ice forming all along the shore, broken only where an ancient derelict wooden boat points its crude square prow toward the open reaches of the lake.

His old Buick sits looking out on the lake with dull eyes. The snow doesn't stick to the waxed black surface except on the trunk and roof and hood. Liv opens the door and thrusts the hen on the floormat in the back seat.

He drives as fast as he dares toward Odin and worries about the dark, the early dark. Through the horizontal veils of snow trailing across the gravel road he sees an old Chevrolet dragging its muddy bottom toward him. Ah, two old men sitting together. Both live in the Roosevelt Hotel in town. The hotel is a monastery of sorts. The hotel is full of old men who play cards and sleep and look out of the lobby window at the street and come down to eat beef commercials at the Square Deal Cafe. Celibate old patriarchs, each in his own room, but not those two. Something else.

The old Chevrolet passes without greeting. Those two—Oyen and Olson. They are not like the others. They are companions, lovers. O and O—orifices of difference.

But Oyen is dying of cancer. Said so matter-of-factly. Came in to get a toothache fixed. His head was stained red-purple—like a huge blear of a birthmark—on one side and the incision was stitched up like a wide, thin upside-down grimace. "Just pull the tooth so it don't hurt so much," Oyen said. "You could take the gold and give it to somebody, I suppose," he said. "I won't have much use for it after a bit," he said.

Olson waited for Liv to finish with Oyen that morning—Olson with the curly white hair and big pink face and pouted mouth and wide, sad gray eyes. Oyen was quick and dark—not a farmer, but a jeweler with hands delicate for watch repair—hands that fluttered like the wings of a pinned bird when he was excited. Together, they had played basketball and such things in high school. Their team pictures were there in a glass case in a hall. They stood, arms over each other's shoulders—Oyen and Olson at the forwards.

Oyen sat in the dental chair that day, waiting for the Novocain to take effect. While Liv stood silently aside, Olson came over to the chair and began to weep and then Oyen's jeweler's hands sought the tears like jewels to hold them awhile. Liv stepped away into another room to hunch his shoulders with the weight of another mystery, before pulling the tooth (inlaid deeply with gold) and putting it into an envelope they left behind with him.

In town Liv takes the mallard into his garage and puts it behind the woodpile and hunches his shoulders on his secret. Savage and illicit it is.

As he drives back toward the lake, the snow is steadily doing its artwork on the fenceposts and strawsheds and hills. At the public landing, when Liv drives in to park, the two of them are sitting close together in the Chevrolet. Liv hurries into boots and shell-belts and feels like a frog in all his mottled green when he is dressed to go and retrieve the other bird.

He cannot resist a final look at them as he stands at the prow of his boat ready to launch it. Their heads are together, a hand curled at one face. He waves. The hand removes, but doesn't wave back.

When he pushes the boat out, the ice cracks and shatters and screeches as its sharp edges cut at the sides of it. As he moves beyond the ice, the waves crash over the prow and Liv turns the boat north, rowing hard for the weeds and the dull bobbing of his dozen and a half decoys. He stops and tries to disentangle two of them because they are making a loud cluk-

cluk noise as they hit together. The decoys are plastic-perfect, their anchor cords gold and weed-tangled where they ray into depth.

Drake. Where is the drake? Liv rows and rows. Above him, swinging off the gray wind towers, the migrating birds set their wings and sail down to rest far, far out on the lake in black rafts from which restless multitudes rise and drop, rise and drop.

The drake rests in a quiet water. His head is velvet green, his legs orange. Liv fears him—even dead. Remembers his rage at being shot, his circling convulsive rage like a clockwork duck, around, around, around. Indignity and now dignity. I will not hunt again, Liv announces to himself. I have killed the swans at Coole, the two. This is not love; this is death.

He pulls the drake from the water. Blood seeps the eyes, the bill. Purple there too—at the neck—and deep white plumage for the north, the ice. What is the secret of the north? Who guides them far down the pathless sky? He covers it with a gunny sack.

Darkness flows steadily down the hills to the west of the lake as Liv hurries to take in the decoys, rowing up to each, pulling it into the boat, winding the anchor cord in. His fingers stiffen with the cold water.

Liv sees the farmhouse lights begin to come on there on the brow of the pine hills. God is not asleep, he muses. He will find me a pillow for my head and wake me through the tall window of his morning. But this is that kind of night, that kind of night. Liv rows toward the shore and aches in his soul for human companionship. The wind is relentless and has tired him out. And he dare not drift too much. Submerged heads of cedar trees are there somewhere past the place he must turn to the landing.

He sees his car, beetle-browed on the little hump of the landing. Turns and the edge of ice screeches at the aluminum sides of the boat. The ice resists. He stands up, pitching the prow up on the ice. Again, again, again. Rocks it and rocks it to break a path through the shell.

It occurs to Liv, because he has not thought to see it, that there is another path parallel to his through the ice—a path of shattered and floating ice fragments already freezing into solidity.

On the shore the old Chevrolet—theirs—sulks beyond his Buick under a low willow, its dark headlights aimed blindly toward the water, its high-humped brown body downing with the snowfall and settling in, settling in.

Where are they?

Liv stands up to see and then he is his own sail. The wind catches him; his hunting coat balloons up under his arms. He scuds backward and lets it happen. There is something to see. The water is shallow. His flashlight beams through the swirl of snow. The water is not deep. It is the silt that is deep—the silk-soft field of fine soil etched by weed and water that is deep.

And, of course, they are there under the wash and wave, green and gray as fish, rocking in one seat of the old boat. They sit together as in an aqueous pew, their legs in the silt. Surely they have stood up and broken the boards and sat down, hand in hand, to bubbly doom. Eros and Omega.

And he leaves them there. He rows numbly back to shore to drag his own boat, rasping on stone and gravel, over to his car. He leaves it there too because he has to call someone to retrieve the two of them, to tug and float them back on shore. In the morning the ice will prevail. You cannot leave them out there in their arctic.

He hurtles the car through torrents of snow, bucking the new little wedge-drifts, the car huff-huffing as it breaks through them.

It takes a long time to call, to explain. The sheriff. Dense man of law. It is like driving toothpicks into ice.

"Where are they again, exactly?" Sheriff Meyer asks, testing Liv, his voice cool and metallic on the phone.

"I have not been drinking, sir," Liv replies. Ah, reputation is no bubble, he muses.

"You couldn't get at them?"

"Should I pull them up like carrots?" Liv asks.

"What time was it when you saw them?"

"When it was very late. Now it's damn near too late forever and you will have to chop them out of the ice," Liv says, "or wait till spring."

"Well...."

"Well, hell! I'll get some farmers with block and tackle and lanterns," Liv says.

"Now don't get carried away," Meyer says. "I've had enough rope tricks with that Unitarian preacher, damn it. I know where it is."

"It's the path through the ice nearest the point," Liv says. "You can't miss them. They are there where the...you'll see where they stopped breaking the ice."

"You be there too," Meyer says.

Liv hangs up and takes two shots of Jack Daniels, blended and aged.

In his garage he turns on the light and picks up the hen mallard and holds it up with the drake. He cannot, for the life of him, figure out what to do with them. "What am I going to do with you?" he asks them. Nothing. Their long bodies dangle at the necks; the orange legs make little flames of cold fire under each. All but one of their fires gone out. He cannot figure out what to do.

He lays them on the still-warm hood of the Buick. Soft is their repose on the liquid waxed black surface.

He goes in to his bedroom and removes all of his hunting clothes and all of his other clothes. God, to be in the sheets of Molly Lee, to hear her heart under a big warm breast beating, to tangle in her summer weeds and mosses, to hear the quacking of her laughter while the wind whistles everywhere around their bed. He could tell her about the two of them—both of the twos—and she would cry for him, for him.

But he knows the sheriff will want to know many things. He talks to his bottle of Jack Daniels. "What do you think about all this, Jack?" he asks. "To hell with the sheriff!" Jack says, and Liv hurries into his dental office where the phone is. Dials. Thank God, the old central, the telephone operator, is gone. Had ears like an elephant.

Ring.

Hoarse hello.

"Molly, this is Liv. I wish to discuss various and sun-dry subjects with you and I wish to not tell the truth with you—that is, in your bed...."

"Then, do come over, Dr. Liv," the voice says. "And if you wish, bring Jack with you."

"Yes, I will," Liv says, standing there numb and naked and red-fuzzed and lank-peckered and shivering. Until he sees the packet with the tooth in it—Oyen's tooth—and then he hurries to get dressed and to walk through the snow on the solid walks through the pine-bearded darkness to her white arms.

Child of Light

The big livestock truck was full of Hovland's bawling Holsteins and he wanted to cry out—to shoot them or the driver or something but he knew that wouldn't do. The driver was a young kid from Odin. He had a wife and a baby and not an ounce of smart aleck in him. He was just trying to make a living and they sent him out from Hayes Trucking to do his job. And then after all Hovland himself helped load the Holsteins just after milking time. So why take it out on the driver—a short boy with freckles and a stout body and a sunburned nose and a lot of worry in his young eyes already.

"It's a shame," the driver said when the eighteen Holsteins were loaded. He didn't look at Hovland as he spoke but sooner or later he would have to when it came time to have Hovland sign the papers.

"They are prime," Hovland said, rubbing the gray whiskers on his long face. "It took me twenty-two years to build up the herd. Now they'll be hamburger down there in Duluth." He stepped back. He was a tall man and he didn't want to loom over the boy.

"I heard they're trying to cut down on milk production," the driver said. He was trying to slip a carbon in under the tally list, but his hands were shaking so hard the carbon slipped away in the breeze and fluttered blackly to the ground.

Hovland retrieved it, took hold of the little tally book and slipped it under the original tally sheet.

"I feel awful," the driver said. "I get about one job like this a month."

"It's not your fault," Hovland said. "I didn't manage right and now

I lose it all. I've had so much stuff hauled away during the last two weeks I'm getting used to it."

"It's a pretty farm," the driver said. "We rent just the buildings on another place the PCA took. There are two acres with the buildings so we got a garden and an orchard."

"You're an Aslesen?"

"Ya."

"You went to school, but you came back."

"Both Carrie and I wanted to stay here, but it's hard—and the town— well it seems to be dying on the edges or something. They closed the Bijou theatre last week. People just rent video tapes now and sit at home and watch by themselves. It's not like going to the show together."

"A farm can die too," Hovland said "...when the people go away from it."

"I have to be rolling," Aslesen said. "Is there anything else left?"

"Just my homemade tractor," Hovland said. "They don't know what to do with it. Nobody bid on it."

"I wonder why," Aslesen said, smiling.

"What?" Hovland asked.

Aslesen spoke louder. "I'll bet nobody who knew you would bid it."

"Maybe," Hovland said. "It's a nice idea anyway. People stay away from you when you're down on your luck."

The cows were bawling and mooing inside the long green and orange trailer and the truck engine sputtered black exhaust smoke up against the outline of the silo. Hovland couldn't quite make them out through the slats and he was glad he could see only slices of black and white patchwork. They were prime all right—meat now. No names. The trailer creaked with their weight.

"Are you going to stay in the buildings?" Aslesen asked. He had a tight, nervous look on his face as he climbed up into the truck cab.

"No, I'm not staying here. I've got everything taken care of...say, you wait. I got something for you."

Hovland saw Aslesen look at his wristwatch so he hurried. My gosh! he said to himself. We've been talking out here like it's all a crime—a sin. But then it is a shame too—everybody's ashamed, I guess.

He found the gun in a case just inside the milk processing shed—a nearly-new Marlin with inletting on the stock and forearm. As he made his way with it towards the driver he couldn't help scowling at himself because the boy looked terrified.

"You take this!" he yelled up at the cab where the driver sat. "It's the last gun. I don't give a damn for guns anymore. You do what you want with it. I can't hunt on my own land so I'm not hunting at all. I don't want to run around asking for permission."

"I can't..."

"Yes, you can." He handed the gun up and when the driver tugged at it, he turned and walked away, a cold laugh forming inside his head.

He took it, Hovland said to himself, because he thinks he's doing me a favor. If I don't have a gun I can't do it—like the others he knows about.

He didn't even turn to wave goodbye to the driver. He just walked away. As he walked toward the tractor shed he heard the truck rev up, its engine howling as the rig creaked and rumbled up the driveway through the aspens and pines. Then it was gone and an awful quiet descended upon the farm.

Because the farm was dead. Oh, yes, the oats waved in the wind on the hill below the grove and the windmill turned and a stray chicken strolled through the cow lot pecking and clucking, but the house was empty and his wife Ellen and daughter and granddaughter were gone to town for boxes—moving boxes. He could imagine their talk.

That granddaughter was something. How could his daughter have an angel like that with a devil of a husband who ran around nights clear over in Bemidji? When she came over to see her grandpa his whole world seemed to fill with light from her hair. Her name was Solveig—the sun—but a different light. Healing. Gentling. Sometimes she combed his hair and played beauty operator like her mother. He saw himself in a mirror once—a long brown face and the knob of a nose—with a silly grin on his face while she combed.

Anyway, his daughter would be soothing Ellen as she drove them to Grand Marais. She would be saying things like, "We mustn't let this tear us all apart." She would be mothering her mother and her mother would be crying a lot and resisting the urge to openly blame him for it all. So some men are good providers; some are not. A man must always take care of things; that is his job. That is his manhood. Then to crawl into town and beg for some work someplace...fixing lawnmowers or selling feed or seed. Oof! Begging. Do you want to buy? Do you want to buy? Selling is begging.

No more indignities.

He smelled his shirt. Cow smell. His head ached and there were voices in it. A farmer is a farmer. So he—Hovland—wore suntans and dress shirts and straw hats—no damn seed corn caps—working in the fields—so he was thought to be a gentleman farmer. Then the proud man falls. He smells of cows and has none. There is manure on his good Red Wing boots but he has no livestock. He removed his straw hat and tried to listen to things outside of his head to cool his mind down.

The farm was dead. Something was gone from it. He killed it.

Oh it looks good. There's a tall red barn with a new shingled roof ($3100—for shingles alone). There's a purple steel silo—the newest—$78,000—at eighteen percent.

Proud. Empty.

They call it over-improvement. His father would not build anything unless he could do it with his own hands. Prospered during the Depression even. A good provider. Admired like a god by a lot of folks.

The sun was beating on his face. A hot day was coming. Through the heat waves off the black-brown cattle lot the fences blurred and moved in slow thermal waves.

The sun was like his father's face—always cheerful, cheerful, but stern too and hard to look into.

He was tired of growing things and of the sun. Growing things wears you out.

There is a coolness someplace without the sun—a cooling, gentle place.

He shook his head and then stood up, thinking about darkness.

They didn't want the barn or milkshed or the silo. They were worth nothing even though they cost him everything.

The sin. What was it?

In the old books about the pioneers they said again and again, "It is a hard thing to move a cow into this country." A caribou—yes—it comes off the land from the north and belongs here in the right season among the cedars and swamps and wet meadows. But a cow—with the udder and the clumsiness—what business does a cow have in the land of deer and caribou? Goats maybe. Even sheep. But to bring a cow across the water—well, that is an unnatural thing. Before there were docks the Swedes simply shoved them off the end of boats and let them swim to shore. There they stood on the purple rocks under the angry gulls, bawling and looking out to sea. They knew better.

Pride too. "Look out how you use proud words," the Swede poet from Illinois said in a book Hovland read in high school.

He did not look at the house. There were no voices there anyway.

There were many boxes stacked in the living room but no voices anymore. No flowers planted this year. Behind the house the cedars his father planted were tall and stern as fathers' beards.

A good time to end it. The wife gets Social Security. She is crabby. "I just papered the living room, you know," she says at least once a day. Doesn't make doughnuts anymore—ever. That was love—doughnuts. The daughter is poor-married to a son-of-a-bitch who doesn't work. There is still the G.I. life insurance though.

Could go into the water. A boat. Take the anchor. Tie it on the neck. Drop in. Let it drift.

The sun burned on his face.

"All right" he cried at the sun. "If that's what you want, then I'll do it." He listened; waited a moment. Nothing.

He walked slowly over to the tractor shed. He did not open the big doors but went in a side door. It was a good building—tightly built. Expensive.

Inside, in the darkness he waited until his eyes let him see. It was cool in there. A dirt floor it had and there was the smell of earth and steel— one soft, one hard and sharp. Yes, a tractor smells when you have worked with it enough, welding and drilling and painting.

The tractor was homemade but it didn't look homemade. He built it for competition at the State Fair. It was a shining blue machine on high, white wheels. Twin exhaust pipes jutted up from a long, lacquered engine compartment and the cab, luxurious with dark-blue cloth seats, rose up into the darkness above the power of the thing. It was an extravagant machine—a giant toy. The engine alone cost $3000. Then there were hundreds of hours of work on the transmission and hydraulic steering and such things. The prize at the Fair was $500. Not much profit there.

He sniffed at his shirt and at the earth floor and the quick, sharp steel of the thing.

It won a prize at Farmfest down in Southern Minnesota just a month ago.

He was proud.

It would be a good way. Nobody wanted either one of them.

He climbed up into the cab and started the engine and sat there. It was comfortable. He wished he could bury himself too, but how could that be done?

The exhaust fumes were acrid and bit at his eyes and at his throat when he breathed.

"No more!" he cried. "No more!"

He pulled the throttle out and let the engine howl and then he himself began to scream until his throat was raw and he could hardly swallow.

Then, suddenly, he saw flowers—a fair little meadow flowing in the darkness. Yellow flowers—flowers of sunshine.

He saw a child's face among the flowers.

"Grandpa! Grandpa!" a child's voice cried. "I can't breathe in here! Please come down!"

"You'll fall!" he cried as she climbed towards him.

He shut the machine off. It was reluctant to stop. It dieseled and popped, shooting hellish sparks up into the darkness of the shed.

Then his granddaughter was sitting on his lap in the cab, coughing and boring into the sockets of her eyes with white little fists. There were hundreds of yellow and white daisies on her dress and they seemed to bloom in his head as he pressed his face into them.

A small hand touched his head and he began to cry.

She talked to him, coughing and explaining.

"I didn't go to town with Mama. I wanted to play with the kitties. 'All right,' Mama said, 'but you find Grandpa and stay away from the barbed wire and the water 'til we get back.' Now you come with me to the house; Mama made potato salad."

He looked at her face in the semi-darkness. Oh, she didn't know, but she would tell and they would know and then she would see the nodding and the looks on their faces and she would know. Grandpa tried to kill himself—that is what she would know.

"I won't tell," she said, stepping gingerly down and finally letting go of his hand.

"I'll tell them all about it," he said, "so your secret won't get to be too much. It's too much for a child." He bent over coughing, then smiled at her.

"Can't you keep the house, Grandpa, so I can come and see you? I know it makes you cry to lose the tractor but it smokes and makes a lot of noise."

"I'll see," he said.

When she opened the shed door a blaze of fierce light blinded him for a moment and he raised his fist into it and swore.

"Oh, don't do that!" she cried. "It scares me." Her little face was serious and looked like she might cry. Then she looked into his eyes and, it seemed, accepted him. Her hand on his was soft and fragile and cool.

He let her lead him toward the house. He felt tired and humble.

"You'll see," she said. "There's lemonade and we'll have potato salad like Mama said we could."

"That would be nice," he said, "but you let me tell them about the tractor and such things. It'll be all right again."

"Well, you come along," she said, not letting go of his hand. "If you come and live in town I can see you a lot. I like it in town."

"I'll think about it," he said, "but let's get out of the sun now."

She was very serious then. "And we'll have potato salad and cookies," she said.

"That sure would be nice," he said. As he walked with her he tried not to see all the emptiness of the place. Rather, he tried to let the two of them fill it with some little joy.

A Trip To Duluth

Seen from the section road running beneath it, the Hoover sisters' farm looked like a quilt of green and gold patchwork except for the house—a little blue Dutch-roofed structure that seemed to cling to the brow of Cedar Ridge like an aphid. The farm had been cleared from the wilderness by their father, who had outlived his wife by twenty years before dying and passing the farm on to his daughters.

The sisters' black Dodge, which they shared driving, had, on that day, been backed out of the garage and stood leaning somewhat sideways as usual on the driveway. People driving by knew that the Hoover "girls," as the two women—both in their seventies—were called, were getting ready to go someplace. In Odin that was news—and people took note of it—not just to be snoopy but to remember to look after things there—*if* the sisters ever managed to get on the road.

If. Why *if*? Why did Chuck Larson and Ewing Lund make bets on such a simple thing when the two Cook County Electric Co-Op linemen passed by in their orange truck and saw the sisters' Dodge sitting outside, its dirty wide-band white sidewalls like smoke rings hung under the fenders.

"Two bucks says never," Larson said, nodding toward the Hoover driveway.

"It's got to be odds," Lund said. "Old Art Jacobsen brought their groceries up yesterday p.m."

"Five to one," Larson said.

"Make it ten."

"Seven to one."

"And they have to get past the Standard station."

"How far?"

"To where they're goin'."

"Well, my gosh, that's Duluth. It ain't even probable."

"All right. Make it Two Harbors."

"And seven to one."

"No, ten to one."

"At a dollar."

"No, two dollars."

"The Highway Patrol ought to put out a bulletin or something the way they aim that old corn sheller down the road."

"Never had an accident."

"But caused a few."

"Never proved it."

"The dead don't say much."

"They ain't so bad."

"Their driving is."

"They got spunk—those old two. I seen both of them swing an ax and pull a saw."

"I seen 'em force a hayrack full of timothy off the road with that car so it tipped over."

"Nobody was hurt."

"Not that time."

"Coffee?"

"You betcha. And I'm lookin' forward to spending my eight bucks."

"Seven."

"They got spunk—the old pioneer spunk...."

"They couldn't make up their mind to do anything as complicated as goin' to Duluth any more than they could make up their mind to marry anyone."

"Were they asked?"

"Well, Jesus, let's get at that transformer. I can see good from up on the pole."

Inside the house up on the hill Clara and Christine Hoover were preparing to pack a lunch after cleaning up the breakfast dishes—thick white plates and heavy stainless steel silverware and a black skillet with a wooden handle. In their appearance and motions the two sisters were virtually twins. Both women were gray and long-boned and hunched over a little and both squinted whenever they looked at anything through their steel-rimmed glasses. Both moved deliberately and carefully, looking where they might step or place things and always making sure they did not bump into each other. Both wore Mackinaw jackets—Clara's red and Christine's green—and jeans and hiking shoes. Through the cooking smells there was also the tense, virile smell of ancient sweat from lean flesh.

"We should leave by 10:00," Christine said, as usual not quite looking at Clara.

Clara did not reply for a long time. During the interval the octagonal oak kitchen clock ticked solemnly.

"The mail doesn't come until 10:30. If we wait too long I have to drive directly into the sun."

"It's my turn to drive," Clara said.

"Well, you got a headache last time we drove in at noon. The sun was right in your eyes."

Clara was cutting slices of bread baked the day before. "What're we going to have for sandwiches?" she asked. She stopped cutting. "We could use that luncheon meat," she added.

"It's going to be a warm day, the radio said."

"We can put some ice cubes in with it."

"It doesn't sound good," Christine said, opening the refrigerator and peering in, her face ghostly in the flash of light.

"What doesn't?"

"Water in the meat."

"How will water get into the meat?"

"Melting. Then it's all spoiled."

Clara chopped at the bread slices lying on the breadboard.

"You aren't cutting them in half, are you?" Christine said, closing the refrigerator door.

"Why not?"

"You know I like to fold the pieces over."

"I'll cut some and leave some."

Christine sat down at the kitchen table across from where Clara was cutting the bread. The sun was shining into the kitchen and beamed on her big, brown hands. She pulled them back off the table and into her lap.

"You're cutting too much, aren't you? It doesn't keep fresh if you slice it."

"It does in the store."

"That's full of preservatives."

"Not Home Bake bread. It says 'no preservatives' on the label."

"I don't believe those labels," Christine said. "They don't care if they ruin your bones or not or give you cancer."

"There's a law about lying on a label."

"Where?"

"It's government."

"We could use some of that roast we made yesterday," Christine said. "Is there enough?"

"Not for both of us," Clara said, scooping up the bread crumbs and putting them back into the plastic sack with the slices of bread and the rest of the loaf.

"The sun is already too high," Christine said.

"All we need to do is put on our sunglasses."

"Those clip-ons scratched my plastic lenses. I had to get new lenses for $129."

"Well, adjust them."

"It seems to me that the logical thing is to take the bread with us to town and buy cold meat in there," Christine said.

"Except that means we'll have processed meat, which is exactly why I wanted to take some ice," Clara said.

"How are we going to keep the ice separate?"

"We'll put it into a plastic bag," Clara said. "Then as it melts it won't go anyplace."

"We'd better check the car," Christine said. "Seems to me it shimmies lately...."

"That was the road south of Hovland," Clara said. "It does that to the car. I didn't notice it last time I drove it."

"Well, Father said if you feel it just in your hands it's a shimmy. If you feel it in your seat and legs it's something else."

"The mail has come," Clara said. "The flag is down."

"Well I hope that boy didn't do it again so you have to walk all the way down there for nothing," Christine said. She paused. "—like last time," she added.

"When was that?"

"Last week."

"That was six weeks ago."

Clara walked around her sister's chair, opened the refrigerator and pushed the full plastic bag into one of the shelves. Then she turned and looked at her sister, her arms folded over one another.

"Don't you look at me that way," Christine said, standing up and folding her arms the same way.

"We'll never get to Duluth at this rate," Clara said, unfolding her arms.

"Well, you wanted to wait for the mail," Christine said, "and then you were slicing and slicing away."

"For heaven's sake!" cried Clara. "I'm going down to get the mail."

"*If* it's there!" Christine called after her.

"Oh, it'll be there, all right," Clara called over her shoulder.

After Clara stepped outside and began the walk down the driveway to the mailbox, Christine walked over to the front window to watch.

"It won't be there," she called through the window to her sister. "You just go ahead, but it won't be there and if it *is* we'll be late getting started and then you'll get a headache from the sun and you'll complain but I won't be listening. You and he always got your way but I just sat back and watched and I got my way too and you didn't even know it, the two of you...."

She could see her sister pulling letters and a catalog from the aluminum mailbox.

"That's mine!" she cried. "That's my catalog so why are you reading it, anyways?"

Clara was walking up the driveway. As she walked, she was thumbing through the Burpee seed catalog.

"You have no right!" Christine cried at Clara. Then she backed away from the window so she wouldn't be caught watching. With a little whimper she turned, stepped into the kitchen and plopped down in a kitchen chair.

"Oh, she'll be just insolent when she comes in, I suppose," Christine said, sitting up straight in the chair.

The outside kitchen door swung open and Clara stepped in, smiling. She still had letters tucked under her left arm.

"Did you drop any?"

Clara laid the catalog on the table. When Christine saw that the edges of the cover were curled up she frowned.

"Any what?"

"Letters."

"No."

Christine stood up, walked into the living room and looked down the driveway. No letters there....

"Only thing for you is the catalog," Clara said, nodding toward where it lay on the table.

"And what did you think of the catalog?"

"What? I haven't read it."

"You don't *read* catalogs."

"I don't."

"They're not like books."   .

"Don't you want to get going?"

"Of course, but don't complain to me."

"About what?"

"Headaches."

"I won't. We'll take the bread along and buy cold meat in town."

"In one of those packages?"

"No, at a real meat market so we'll get just enough."

Clara pulled the sack of bread out of the refrigerator and put it into a larger grocery sack. "I'm going to check the car," she said.

"Well, how can you check the shimmy standing still?"

"Tell you what," Clara said. "If it shimmies, I'll pay for fixing it."

"Oh, it shimmies all right. You'll see. It's in the hands...."

"I'm going out," Clara said.

"Any thunderstorms coming?"

Clara turned, her big brown hands on the edge of the door. "What?"

"You know how the windshield wipers work."

"They work fine. If it rains too hard we'll pull over."

"The Engebretsons did that and a truck hit them. Both have terrible headaches now from whiplash."

"It's not supposed to rain," Clara said, slamming the door.

"Same as Father," Christine muttered. "He just walked out the door on Sunday morning and you had to run after him just like a little puppy or get left behind."

She stood up and went into the bathroom and began looking for something. She went through everything—every bottle. Then she went into the kitchen and looked in a cabinet where they sometimes kept things like antacid and aspirin.

She heard the horn beep and jumped. "You wait!" she muttered. "You just wait."

When Clara opened the kitchen door her face was flushed and her eyes, finally, began to focus on Christine. Behind her, through the open door, the engine of the old Dodge was idling noisily, its tappets clat-clatting, its big headlights peering blankly at the kitchen door.

"What on earth is keeping you?" Clara yelled over the noise.

Christine bent over and began to weep quietly. Then she raised her head and said, "I was looking for some Excedrin for your headache."

"What headache?"

"You'll *get* one. You always do."

"We can buy some on the way."

"Those little places charge twice as much."

"I give up," Clara cried, shrugging her shoulders and then leaning wearily against the door.

"Now it's my fault."

"Maybe it is."

"We need a vacation from each other," Christine said.

"That's how *you* feel. It's been too long together for you."

"I didn't say that," Christine said.

Clara's voice softened. "Couldn't we just make an adventure of it or something? Just jump in the car and go?"

Christine slumped in her chair. "I'm all worn out," she said. "I need a nap. Maybe it's that new prescription...."

"Oh, it's not new," Clara said.

"Now you're mad at me."

"No, I'm not," Clara said. "I'm too tired to get mad now."

"I've tired you out so it's my fault," Christine said. "You told me to tell you my needs but when I do you get upset with me." She was crying again.

"It's all right," Clara said. "I'll turn the car off and make us some hot chocolate. It's already past lunch time."

"We could have the garage check the car this afternoon."

"All right," Clara said. "Then at least we'll get something done today besides warming the motor up."

"You want to call the garage?"

"It was your idea."

"My idea so I'll be paying the bill too, I suppose."

"Tomorrow we'll do it then," Clara said. She walked out and drove the car into the garage. It died with a gasp and a wheeze. When Clara came back in, Christine had the teapot on and was slicing some roast beef onto bread slices—full ones for her; half ones for Clara.

Down below the sisters' house, Larson, the Cook County Electric Co-Op Lineman, leaned back on the wide leather belt that held him to the pole, dug his hooks in and laughed.

"You owe me seven dollars!" he yelled down to Lund.

"The day isn't over yet!" Lund yelled back up at him.
"For them it is!" Larson cried.
"We never settled the odds!" Lund yelled.
"Yes we did: seven to one."
"No we didn't. *You* did maybe, but I didn't."
"The hell we didn't!" Larson yelled.
"We just settled the Two Harbors part."
"What're you tryin' to pull anyways?"
"We never settled the odds, that's what...."

Mowing the Cemetery

Liv awakens and wonders vaguely through the sullen throbbing of his enormous hangover if it is perhaps resurrection day. The sun is slanting rays of long cathedral light up through the gaunt cemetery cedars and across the pink and gray and white headstones. Polished marble gleams. Inscriptions write themselves out of shadows, expectant.

A striped gopher—perfectly erect as Liv is (inside his wrinkled pants)—sticks up from the grass. It occurs to Liv that the gopher is gopher-toothed, in need of orthodontia. He cough-laughs. The gopher spasms into his hole.

Liv turns on his back and searches for the morning star through the haze inside his eyes. It is there—wan and pale, dissolving into fiercer light. Oh, the things one is promised in the morning!

It is not resurrection day, of course: it is merely morning and Liv is lying on the grass between two graves on a little rise in the Lutheran cemetery. Pocket gophers are tunneling a few feet away, creating little round mounds of freshly-dug earth. Down on the other end of the cemetery the sexton is already digging another grave with shovel and pickax. "Check! Check! Check!" the pickax goes. It is not resurrection day.

The rind of a used condom hangs on the laced limb of a cedar, thrown there during the night. The fruits of love; the husks of love. The sexton will see it and remove it. Cannot have it dangling there during an interment. Yet it too, is mortality, a spurt in a Sheik—a little moaning death. At that moment both probably gazed with bulging, transfixed eyes over each other's shoulders at the stones. Peter. *Tu Est Petrus.*

Dandelions begin to wink at Liv, jesting with the sun. Liv knows they are wise to him and he winks painfully back, his eyes sore and blearing.

Liv's erection begins to go down. He should have been in bed with Molly Lee and then gone from mourning into morning with her. He doesn't remember where he has been. Night music, dance and the wind roaring in the cedars are in his head. Night music plays in distant regions behind his eyes where his heart hears it. Hoo! Hoo! Hoo! It is the Hardanger fiddle of Jonas Lee, the brother of Molly. Jonas is not playing at some *where* or *when*. He keeps playing in the heart's memory. Memory is an affliction, is it not?

The Norwegian Hardanger fiddle has two sets of paired strings—one for the notes of the melody; the other for sympathetic vibration. And so the fiddle sounds like geese honking on the migratory wind for the regions where the ship of the sun (The Flyer) passes closer to the earth. There is joy in such migration, but then there is also the other echo—the plaint for the north, for the place of flapping love and gosling nest and feeding with joyful celebration of the appetites. All music plays—*inter vivos*—against the deep vibrations of mortality, the second string, the lower string. The stars begin to fade. Day insists on time.

He turns and lies on his left side so he can see the town. Odin, irony. The Unitarian preacher hanged like the old Norse god. Well, the town yawns in windows and doors, stretches on sidewalk and street and wakes up in the grass. Those who lie late in bed and regard the yellow tolling of light think on the old questions. How much has the grass grown during the night? Where is it now? Does it tangle the roses we have set out? It wants us to lie down again. It will someday whisper our windows asleep and tickle the sawn boards until they, too, will lie down around us, curling like long brown leaves.

Liv wonders who he is that the fiddle plays such ancient music in his soul.

There in the town is dentist Liv's temple—Athens in Minnesota—a bank in the Greek revival style—of this time, of that place. Under the lamp above his dental chair—they will sit with mouths yawned and aghast, taking his gold, his silver, his hard truth. And damn them, the ingrates will not pay him until they are good and ready, if then. So how will he continue to pay his bills?

Here is Mayor Liv surveying his little kingdom on the side while, behind him down a slant of morning light, Richard Lee, Molly Lee's other brother, starts his smoky mowing, knowing Liv is up there lying between the graves of two pastor's wives gone down. Infidelities. What is the joke?

He is reported—the pastor—to have said, "Plant me right between them—an equal distance between each, but you might discreetly tilt me just a degree or so toward Martha." Yes, they all think they're wise to you.

The Luther Memorial Home—there on the edge of town. Forty rooms and forty tubes of Deep Heat and the smell of the bones. But some climb up in the sheets and dance their dance. Good little deaths. Hooray for the amorous old farts. Connubial embraces, kind hearts, coronaries.

The school is summer empty—the school where children sing and many show that through the braces, the rubber bands, Liv has given them a smile for the time when they are still young and easy.

Has given. Too much is expected of him.

The courteous mower approaches behind him. The condom dangles its slick pink husk on the evergreen. The grass waits; dandelions nod wisely. The town waits.

Too much is expected of him.

Yet, for a little while, until the October, his green heart beats in its cage and the fiddle plays its sweet-sad music.

He gets up to go back to his duties. He has many appointments to meet. He salutes with a shaking right hand the citizenry of the place. Here's to you old patriarch and you young mother and you child. When we are born heaven lies about us; soon the rest of the world begins to lie about us too.

He relieves himself behind a cedar. Good whiskey to waste. The sun warms him; warms the stones, his purple cock. Zips. Sighs. Steps over Martha's grave, gravely.

On the edge of town, marble dawn.

The Author

John Solensten, a native of Minnesota, graduated from Gustavus Adolphus College and served in the U.S. Army in Korea. He taught English in South Dakota where his novel *Good Thunder* is set, later earned his doctorate in English at Bowling Green University and taught at Mankato State University. His first collection of short stories is *The Heron Dancer*. Solensten has also written three plays that have been produced and he edited *There Lies A Fair Land*, an anthology of Norwegian-American writing. Currently he teaches literature and writing at Concordia College in St. Paul, Minnesota, and describes himself as a "regionialist" with a fascination for small-town American life.

The Artist

Robert Walton is a native of South Dakota, received degrees from Augustana and the University of North Dakota, taught in West St. Paul, Moorhead and now teaches art in the Fargo Public Schools. His art reflects the people and landscape of the Upper Midwest. His work has been exhibited from Winnipeg to Kansas. He currently lives in Moorhead, Minnesota.

LONE BUTTE PRESS